WHY ISN'T
BECKY TWITCHELL
DEAD?

ALSO BY MARK RICHARD ZUBRO:

A Simple Suburban Murder

Why Isn't Becky Twitchell Dead?

Mark Richard Zubro

CHICAGO HEIGHTS PUBLIC LIBRARY

St. Martin's Press
New York

WHY ISN'T BECKY TWITCHELL DEAD? Copyright © 1990 by Mark Richard Zubro. All rights reserved. Printed in the United States of America. No part of this book may be used or reproduced in any manner whatsoever without written permission except in the case of brief quotations embodied in critical articles or reviews. For information, address St. Martin's Press, 175 Fifth Avenue, New York, N.Y. 10010.

Design by Judy Dannecker

Library of Congress Cataloging-in-Publication Data

Zubro, Mark Richard.
    Why isn't Becky Twitchell dead? Mark Richard Zubro.
        p.   cm.
    ISBN 0-312-03887-9
    I. Title.
    PS3576.U225W4   1990
    813'.54—dc20   89-48534

First Edition
10 9 8 7 6 5 4 3 2 1

For my brothers Jim and John

6-19-90 B&T 15.95

◢◣ Acknowledgments ◢◣

For their kindness, patience, and assistance, I wish to thank Tim Dailey, Tonia Gurnea, Mike Kushner, Mike Moustis, Rick Paul, Kathy Pakieser-Reed, and especially Peg Panzer and Sara Paretsky.

Mark Richard Zubro
June 1989
Mokena, Illinois

WHY ISN'T
BECKY TWITCHELL
DEAD?

1

I hate grading spelling tests. Quizzes, essays, book reports, even twenty-page research papers I don't mind. Somewhere in the seventh circle of hell, the doomed English teachers slave away for eternity grading spelling tests. No fate could be worse.

A cold Monday in late December and I wanted to go home. But I felt guilty because I'd delayed grading the damn things for over two weeks already. Under the pile of spelling tests lurked a stack of senior essays waiting to be graded.

I sighed and grabbed another stack. Scott wasn't due to pick me up for another hour, anyway.

Erratic noises drifted in from the corridor. At first, I presumed one of the janitors had been overcome with a mad desire to move a mop from one storage closet to another. Nothing ever seemed to get cleaner at Grover Cleveland High School. They built the main portion just before World War I. The school looks as if it hasn't been cleaned since just prior to World War II. A janitorial staff of even average competence could at least cover the major flaws after all these years. I gave a sour look to the back wall of my classroom. What used to be a few flakes of plaster forming charming patterns as they fell threatened to turn into a gaping entry into the science room next door. Science being even worse than spelling, I shuddered at the possible merger.

The noises grew closer. I heard loud voices punctuated by angry bellows and stomping feet.

I strolled to the door. Mrs. Trask and a male janitor approached. He saw me and grumbled about parents not being allowed in the building without permission, but that if I was here, it was probably all right. Throwing spiteful looks at her back, he retreated. I invited Mrs. Trask into my classroom. Today, she wore electric green trousers under a maroon woolen overcoat. Her thin blond hair swirled in greater disarray than usual.

She said, "Mr. Mason, Jeff's been arrested."

She had two boys—Eric and Jeff. The older, Eric, is the dumbest person I have dealt with in all my years of teaching. Forget this nice bullshit about how he was "slow, disadvantaged, socio-economically deprived," or any other pet name. He was dumb. I knew it. He knew it. I never threw it in his face, just helped him cope. When I had him as a freshman six years ago last September, what he scrawled on a piece of paper could have been generously ascribed to a human being. By June of that year, what he wrote contained definite signs of punctuation at the ends. Most fair-minded observers would say that the enlargements at the beginnings resembled capital letters.

Even the stuff between the enlargements and the punctuation could be said to resemble words, not necessarily from any language known to me but close enough. Besides, I had more success with him than any teacher'd had in five years.

Mrs. Trask checks in as the second dumbest person I've dealt with as a teacher—not counting administrators. I suspect that she is illiterate. I've never seen her read one of the notes or letters teachers and social workers have sent her. She's approached me numerous times, asking me to explain what a note from a teacher really meant. Her good-heartedness approached the embarrassing sometimes—always remembering certain teachers' birthdays with little cakes dropped off in the office;

constantly willing to help but fearful of intruding. In many ways, in bringing up her boys on her own she floundered out of her depth; but she knew what was best according to her lights and never compromised what she thought was right.

The first time I helped her bail Eric out of jail had cemented us as friends forever. I liked her barrel-shaped dowdiness. It was her, with no apologies to anyone.

Her first time in juvenile court in front of a cynical and uncaring judge had cured her of easy sentiment regarding her boys. Eric's the only kid who ever tried to take a swing at me. Mrs. Trask told me I should have decked her kid. Now he keeps my eight-year-old Chevette in more than reasonable working order.

Mrs. Trask and I had fought side by side as a succession of administrators, sociologists, counselors, and psychiatrists had tried to convince her how rotten Eric was.

"He's stupid, and he's ugly," she said at one point, "and they don't like him because he's extra work and disproves all their bullshit theories, but he's not as bad as they claim."

She was partly right. In all the years I'd dealt with slow kids, you could be dumber than a mud fence, but as long as you were a handsome boy or a pretty girl, you got passed to the next grade. If you were blond, it was even better. It isn't fair, but teachers are as human and hypocritical as everybody else.

Jeff, the child announced as arrested, I now had as a senior in my class of remedial readers. He was reasonably dumb, probably more attributable to years of laziness than to any educational deficiency. He had a wicked sense of humor. I found myself laughing at his stories and jokes more than is recommended in the university-education courses.

Feet planted solidly apart, her coat misbuttoned in haste, Mrs. Trask explained that the police had gone to their home around 3:30 that afternoon. "They slammed Jeff up against the wall, handcuffed him, and dragged him away. It was awful."

"Did they say what happened?" I asked.

"You know the police around here," Mrs. Trask said. "If your kid's been in trouble once, they always think the worst of him."

I knew Jeff had had several run-ins with the River's Edge cops, mostly concerning teenage rowdiness rather than actual criminal behavior.

Mrs. Trask showed the first signs of anger as she explained further. When she's angry enough, I've known her to be able to stand off a crew of burly police sergeants.

"They accused my boy of murder."

I drew in a deep breath, stood up a little straighter.

"His girlfriend, that Susan Warren, they found her dead. They think my Jeff did it. I told them that was stupid. They wouldn't listen to me. You've helped me with these cops before. You know how to talk to them. Could you come with me? I guess you might be busy, but if . . ." Her voice trailed away.

"I'll do what I can, but you need a lawyer for this. It's more serious than the other times. I don't think we'll be able to post bail, if they'll even allow it."

"I just want to talk to my boy. Find out what's going on. See if he's all right."

I agreed to accompany her to the police station. I didn't have my car. Eric had been working on it for three days. His prognosis for its eventual return to health was not good.

I called home. Scott didn't answer. I left a message on the machine so he wouldn't come pick me up.

River's Edge is one of the oldest southwestern suburbs of Chicago, founded soon after Blue Island. From its outward appearance, you'd guess the police station was the first building erected after the founding. Dirty faded bricks—probably originally yellow—crept around the two-story disaster area. Gutters along the north side of the building hung at crazy angles. Around the outside of the building, shattered glass, broken bottles, and rusted beer cans decorated the mounds of dirty unshoveled snow, remnants of a mid-December blizzard. The janitors here must come from the same union as the ones at the high school. Warped shutters nailed haphazardly closed over the first-floor windows added appropriate touches of dreariness. The inside continued the dumpiness scheme begun outside. The walls needed painting. Scratches and nicks beyond counting scored the solid mahogany admitting counter. The smell of mold and mildew struck offensively as we hurried in from the below-zero temperatures.

The cop behind the desk fit right in. He saw us, put down his newspaper leisurely, stood up, hitched his belt over his sixty-year-old paunch, and harrumphed slowly over to us. He walked as if his muscles were as wrinkled as his face. Retirement had to be a day or two away.

A small crowd of kids from school huddled in one corner. Among them, I recognized Becky Twitchell and Paul Conlan. They approached me and Paul Conlan asked, "Mr. Mason, what's going on?"

"I'm here to help Jeff," I answered.

Abruptly Becky yanked him away and the rest of the group followed them.

The cop refused to let us see Jeff. He couldn't or wouldn't tell us anything about the case. I asked to talk to Frank Murphy. He wasn't available.

Frank and I used to work together with troubled kids when he was in the juvenile division, before he got transferred to homicide. We'd enjoyed numerous successes with some very tough kids.

I drummed my fingers indecisively on the countertop. The cop retreated to his newspaper. Mrs. Trask looked ready for a major assault on the duty cop. The entry of a short potbellied man dressed in baggy coveralls, flannel shirt, and slouch hat forestalled her annihilation of a suburban police station.

The man ignored us, marched to the counter, slammed his fist on the top, and demanded to see whoever was in charge.

5

The ancient cop behind the counter rolled his eyes upward, shuffled to his feet, and began another trek from his desk to the counter. When he got there, the cop pulled at his lower lip a minute while he waited for the red-faced guy to shut up and draw a breath. After his face achieved a curious state of purple, the guy stopped. The cop asked him his name.

"Jerome Horatio Trask," was the bellowed reply, followed by more demands and outrage.

A few curious uniformed cops peered from around doorways. The old cop sighed. He pointed to us. "Wait with them," he muttered.

Trask looked where he pointed, turned several more shades of purple, and began another set of protests.

However, the cop had already begun the long journey back to his desk. Trask raved at an indifferent back for a minute. He twisted around, perhaps hunting for support, then stormed over to us.

Upon reaching us, he began verbally abusing Mrs. Trask. His comments centered on what a rotten mother she was. Mrs. Trask bore the attack with a grim frown until he called her a cheap whore and said the boys probably weren't his, anyway.

Mrs. Trask waved her fist in his face. "Get out, you son of a bitch!" Her bellow attracted a mob of cops. Before the crowd could react, he slapped her. I could have told him that was a mistake. In seconds, he lay on the floor. She sat on top of him, pummeling him none too gently into insensibility. His shouted threats turned to strangled yelps. A woman police officer got hold of Mrs. Trask and dragged her off him. With the help of the cop behind the desk, I got hold of Mr. Trask.

I'd never met Mr. Trask. Many's the time I'd gotten an earful from Mrs. Trask about what a rotten human being he was. He drank. He cheated on her. He couldn't hold a job. I could add that he didn't use deodorant. At the moment, he held the side of his jaw with his right hand; his left gingerly probed a rapidly growing blue and black mound around his left eye.

The cops led a slightly disheveled but generally unhurt Mrs. Trask to a women's room to put herself back together. We put Mr. Trask into a chair and let him moan.

Frank Murphy walked down the stairs. He wore the same dark-blue rumpled suit I'd seen him in a hundred times before. He beckoned me over. We exchanged brief pleasantries. The desk sergeant tottered over and explained the recent fracas.

"Keep the two of them apart," Frank told him. He took me to a gray, cheerless room. A scarred and battered table and two chairs sat forlornly in the center. The clanking radiator threatened to turn the room into a sauna. We sat on opposite sides of the table. He took off his glasses and rubbed his eyes. He sighed deeply, then began twirling his glasses in his right hand. He said, "Even you, Tom, are not going to be able to rescue this kid. He's guilty. We've got him cold."

"What happened?"

"We found the girl around ten last night. She was a few feet from the railroad tracks near Eightieth Avenue and One Hundred and Eighty-first Street. She'd been strangled and beaten up worse than I've ever seen. Her right arm was broken in several places and mangled as if someone had tried to twist it off. They found bloody snow all around the body. The medical examiner said she might have been raped. We found her purse nearby with her I.D. inside. She wasn't robbed. We think she must have died sometime after eight, but we're still working on the exact time." He put his glasses back on.

"That's horrible," I said. "The poor kid, who could do something that awful?"

He shrugged. "We think the boyfriend did it." The rest of the story was fairly simple. An engineer on a passing freight reported something suspicious. They sent somebody to investigate. She'd been killed somewhere else and taken to the tracks. The body wouldn't have been discovered for a while if it hadn't been for the engineer. He finished, "She was three or four months pregnant and high on coke."

"Why arrest Jeff?"

"We got bloodstains in his car and on his clothes. They match the dead girl's. He admits to fighting with her last night. He can't account for his movements at the time of the murder."

"Can I talk to him?"

"I've got to get this chaos out front settled first. His public defender was supposed to be here by now. We'll have to check with him."

The scene at the front desk needed only machine-gun emplacements to complete an armed-camp effect. A young female cop and Mrs. Trask huddled at one end of the room. Mr. Trask, a burly male cop with a tattoo of a sailing ship on his arm, and the old guy from behind the desk scowled at each other in another corner.

A dapperly attired gentleman stood between the two groups resting his arm on the counter. His bored look told the world he'd been through this a million times. He introduced himself to Frank as Jeff's public defender.

The warring camps began to make stirring noises. Frank forestalled a resumption of hostilities by asking the lawyer and Mr. Trask to join him in the interrogation room He told Mrs. Trask she would be next. Frank didn't uninvite me, so I tagged along. The lawyer and I stood against the wall on either side of the door to the room. Frank and Mr. Trask sat at the table. Frank introduced us all.

Trask burst out, "I want to know what the hell is going on here. Why have you arrested my boy? What right do you have holding him?"

"Mr. Trask," Frank began.

Trask thumped his fist on the table. "It's all his goddamn mother's fault, anyway. The kid's been trouble since he was five. She babies him. What he needs is some fast kicks on his backside. Then he'd know who was boss. That's what all these kids need today, if you ask me."

Frank said, "Mr. Trask, when's the last time you saw your boy?"

"My wife only lets me visit him once a month. I've been busy lately. I drive a truck long-distance. But that doesn't mean I don't know my boy." He thumped his fist against his chest. "He picked me last summer. He stayed three months. I knew this Susan Warren. You can't hide the kind of reputation she had. She filled him with all kinds of crazy notions. Don't get me wrong, I'm sorry she's dead, but facts are facts. He's better off with her gone."

"What kind of reputation did she have?" the lawyer asked.

"Slut. Whore. Ask any of Jeff's friends. They'll tell you."

"Who told you?"

"I don't memorize shit like that. You hear it around. You hear it enough, you know it's true."

"What crazy notions did she give him?" I asked.

"Trips alone for the two of them. Jeff used to concentrate on sports. He could get into a good college if these goddamn teachers would give him a break now and then. He's a good enough athlete to be a pro someday." He punctuated his tirades with waving fists. He told us that because of Susan, Jeff had talked about getting married right after graduation. Mr. Trask knew guys were supposed to be interested in girls at this age. He was sure his son was no virgin. Mr. Trask knew what it was like to be horny on a Saturday night. At that point, we got a leer and a loud manly chuckle as he said, "I mean, sure I wanted to get my rocks off when I was a teenager, but I kept my head. I didn't let some passing skirt keep me from my goals."

"Did you tell him that?" Frank asked.

"Sure. I've got no secrets from my sons. We get along great. We're buddies. My boys confide in me. I've been to lots of Jeff's games, as many as I could, since way back when he started in fifth grade."

For all of Mr. Trask's fabled closeness to his son, he could give us no account of the boy's recent activities, including the status of his relationship with Susan. He ended the conversation with demands to see his son.

Frank told him they'd interview Mrs. Trask, talk it over with the lawyer, with Jeff, and get back to him. Mr. Trask adjusted his overalls, grabbed at his crotch, and walked out the door, grumbling that there'd better be some action around here pretty soon.

Frank returned with Mrs. Trask. Her firm-set jaw gave solid evidence that she was ready to take on a Marine battalion. I wouldn't have wanted to be the Marines.

She asked quietly, "When can I see my son?"

Frank explained the entire process that would take place. At the end, he said that bail, if granted, would be extremely high.

She blanched when she heard the amount it might take to free her son, then rallied quickly. I patted her arm sympathetically.

"I want to see him," she said.

The lawyer, Frank, and the parents worked out logistics. Frank left to talk to Jeff. He came back with a puzzled expression on his face.

He pointed to me. "He wants to see you."

"Why?" I asked.

Frank shrugged.

"He doesn't want to see me?" Mrs. Trask asked.

"No, ma'am, I'm sorry. He doesn't want to see his father, either."

Mrs. Trask sat thoughtfully. Her puzzled look changed to one of confidence. "I'm willing to trust Mr. Mason, but I'd like to at least try and see him. Can you do that much?"

"If we let you see him, we'll have to let your husband in."

"I can control myself, you just keep that son of a bitch out of my way."

Sorting out who got to see whom when took some delicate

negotiations, but in fifteen minutes, six of us jammed into the room.

Jeff eyed us all suspiciously. After placing the lawyer in charge and warning the parents to observe the truce or face arrest themselves, Frank left.

Jeff wore faded jeans torn at the knees. His hair, usually moussed to spiky straightness, leaned over in sporadic sworls. He wore a black Iron Maiden T-shirt. He sat in the room's other chair. The lawyer and I remained near the entrance.

As soon as the door closed, Mr. Trask began to pace the floor and berate his son.

At first, the lawyer, a Mr. Dwyer, tried to shut Trask up. Nothing worked. Most of Trask's accusations played on the themes of "Look what this girl did to you" or "You should have listened to me."

Three times, Dwyer tried to start a reasonable discussion. For one of the rare moments in my life, I almost felt sorry for a lawyer.

Mrs. Trask eyed her husband with contempt but remained silent.

After five minutes of listening to his dad, Jeff turned to face him. He said very quietly, "Shut the fuck up."

Mr. Trask bellowed in rage and launched himself at his son. Jeff leapt to his feet, sending the chair crashing against the wall. They grappled briefly. Dwyer grabbed Trask. I held on to Jeff. Mrs. Trask didn't move. She sat with a satisfied smile on her face.

Frank Murphy rushed in. "What the hell's going on here?" he asked.

After a few seconds, Jeff ceased struggling. I released my grip on him. An angrily red Trask demanded to be left alone with his son.

"Keep that stupid shit away from me," Jeff said. "I'd rather be in a cell than be alone with him."

Dwyer stood in front of Trask, forestalling another attack. Jeff said, "I asked to speak to Mr. Mason alone."

Mr. Trask erupted again. Jeff shoved his hands into his pants pockets and looked down. After his dad finished fulminating, Jeff said to the floor, "I'd like to talk with Mr. Mason. Just me and him."

"What about me, Jeff?" his mom asked.

Jeff looked as stubborn but less combative than he had with his dad. "I'm sorry, Mom. A little later, but I've got to talk to Mr. Mason."

She stood up, faced me. "Be kind to my boy," she said, and left.

Frank got Mr. Trask and the lawyer straightened out. When only Frank, I, and the boy were left, Frank said, "Tom, this is extraordinary even for you." He eyed me carefully.

I remembered the time we'd stood together over the body of a seventeen-year-old honor student with a full scholarship to Harvard, a popular football player who'd committed suicide minutes before we'd arrived to stop him. I read the years of trust in Frank's eyes. "Do what you can," he said, and left.

I sat on the table.

Jeff paced the room. "I hate him," he said. He stopped and turned to me. "Why did I have to get an asshole for a dad?" He picked up the chair, placed it next to the table, and folded himself into it. He looked up at me. "What's going to happen to me?"

"I don't know."

His shoulders slumped. He rested his elbows on his knees, swung his hands. "I didn't kill her," he stated.

I nodded and waited, let the silence build, then asked, "Why did you want to see me?"

"You're the only one I can talk to. I know what you did for Eric. He swore me to secrecy. He's never told anybody else, don't worry."

Why Isn't Becky Twitchell Dead?

Over the years, some students had distorted my role in helping troubled kids. I know I have a dual reputation: one as an ex-Marine, a mini-Rambo, the other as a strict, boring English teacher. I preferred the latter to the former, and I knew which one was closer to reality. As for Eric: Outside the McDonald's on 159th Street one July evening, the cops had searched him for a kilo of crack I'd convinced him to hand over not five minutes before. I wasn't searched, and I kept my mouth shut. It would've meant a stretch in Stateville if the cops had found the drugs on the boy. I flushed the drugs down the nearest toilet while they interrogated the kid.

I decided to start with something simple. "Tell me about you and Susan, when you met, that kind of stuff."

Jeff fidgeted in the chair, tapped his foot on the floor, and began cracking his knuckles. He scratched at an ugly pimple on his neck, a few inches below his ear. Finally, feet planted on the floor, hands resting on his widespread knees, he began.

They'd attended the same grade school, but hadn't gotten to know each other until the end of sophomore year. They dated that summer, and started going steady Christmas a year ago. "At first, it was great. She didn't make me nervous. I liked being around her. She listened to my stories."

"What happened after 'at first'?"

"I guess I have to tell you because it's all connected with last night." He sighed, then continued. After a while, she'd changed, especially when she was with her friends. They'd laugh and make fun of him, tease him mercilessly. When they'd get alone, she'd keep teasing and then begin to nag and pick at him. He'd get pissed off, but she wouldn't stop. They'd end up screaming at each other. Then one time, she'd slapped him, and he'd hit her back.

He stopped the story. His eyes roved around the room worriedly, then came back to rest on mine. "Do I have to tell all this stuff?"

"Your choice. If you think I can help you without it, or if it's too embarrassing, fine. You decide. I suspect the police or your lawyer will need to hear all of it eventually."

He gulped and then went on. The first time they'd hit each other, they'd said they were sorry and had made up that night. He couldn't look at me as he told the next part. "At the end of our dates, we usually made out for a while. We did that night, but it was as if the hitting each other made a difference. That night we went . . ." He stopped.

I waited a beat, then finished for him. "All the way for the first time."

He nodded and resumed. "The next weekend, I wanted to do more than make out. You know. Do it again. She said no. We had a fight. Worse than before. She tried to slap me, but I grabbed her arm. She laughed at me. She made me so goddamn mad. We wrestled. I hit her a couple more times. She cried a lot. So did I." His face turned red. He scratched at the zit again.

"Stop picking at that," I said.

He looked at his hand guiltily. "Sorry," he mumbled, then continued. "We made up and went all the way again. After a while, it got so I wanted to hit her. I knew it was wrong, but something would come over me. I wanted us to fight so I could get mad, and I knew we'd do it."

"Did you ever discuss the fights with her calmly? Not on a date? When there was a chance you wouldn't fight?"

"I tried. She said she didn't want to talk about it, threatened to break up with me. I still wanted to go out with her. I knew what we did, the hitting and stuff, wasn't right. I wanted to stop. Then on our next date, we'd go through it all again."

"Did either of you drink or do drugs on your dates?"

"We didn't do this stuff because we were drunk or high. We wanted to. The most we ever had was a few beers, maybe a couple hits of dope if somebody else had some."

"What happened yesterday?"

He drew a deep breath. "Yesterday started out okay. We went to Paul Conlan's house to watch football and party."

Paul Conlan lived the life of a cliché—star athlete in three sports, wealthy parents, handsome, popular.

"Paul's my best friend. Seven of us showed up. I wanted to talk to her. I wanted to stop the fights even if it meant no sex. Even if it meant breaking up. I couldn't take the fighting anymore."

He stood up and began to pace around the room. His untied tennis shoes flopped on his feet. He said, "I told her I wanted to leave early. She asked what for. I couldn't tell her in front of her friends. She and her buddies started teasing me. Even the guys joined in. I saw the whole thing starting all over." He leaned against the wall and thumped his fists against his thighs. "I memorized what I was going to say. But all the teasing and hassling pissed me off. When we got in the car to drive to my house, I hated her. I told her it was over between us."

"What'd she say?"

"I think she must have figured that was the excuse for that night's fight. I tried to stay calm. I told her I was serious. That the fights were over. I even pulled to the side of the road and tried to explain. She laughed at me, hit me, slapped me. I tried to stop her."

He walked over to me, head down, his hands out, pleading for understanding. "I hit her. Harder than ever before. She was unconscious. I got real scared." He sat down and told the rest. He drove to a gas station to get some water. She came around but wouldn't talk to him. Susan then spent fifteen minutes in the women's room. When she came out, she ignored him and began walking away. He followed her and offered to drive her home or to a friend's. She pushed him away, then swore at him and started swinging. He claimed he didn't touch her or even lift a hand against her. He knew he couldn't hit her. He said that by then he was crying, begging her to stop, to listen. Finally, she told him he was an asshole jock, and aimed a last kick. He tried to dodge, but she got him in the nuts. While he bent over, she laughed at him, slapped him with her purse, and took off running. He didn't see her again.

After he finished, he slumped down in the chair. I asked a few questions on details.

He drove around until one in the morning. He had no witnesses for this. He sneaked into the house, avoiding his mom, who'd fallen asleep on the couch. At home, Paul Conlan had left a message for him to call no matter when he got in. He'd called Conlan, who had a private phone in his bedroom. Paul told him they'd found Susan dead. One of the kids at the party had seen the police cars at Susan's house and called Conlan. Paul told Jeff the police were hunting for him. Jeff guessed he'd be suspected, figured he'd better not hang around the house. He thought he'd try to hide at a friend's.

I told him about seeing the kids in the police station earlier. He snorted contemptuously. "They wouldn't help last night when I needed them." He continued the story. He couldn't stay at home, he was sure the police would be there. He didn't want the hassle he knew he'd get from his mom. He drove around most of the night. He tried a couple friends. No one, including Conlan, would let him in. He watched for his mom to leave for work, then he entered the house. He didn't answer the phone or the door, but his mom went home at noon and found him. She got mad when he wouldn't talk to her, then later the police arrived.

I asked him about Susan's blood in his car.

"In the fight, she got a bloody nose. They found my blood, too." He rolled his sleeve up and showed me the gouges on his wrist and arm. "The police don't believe I didn't do it."

He claimed to know nothing about Susan's activities after she'd left him. I tried various questions from different angles, but he stuck to his story. Finally, I asked whether there was anything else he could tell me.

He hesitated. "One odd thing last night. After I called Paul, before I left the house, Becky Twitchell phoned. She almost woke up my mom. Becky told me to keep my mouth shut about the kids at the party. She warned me not to tell. You can't be too careful with Becky. Bad things happen to people who cross her."

If they ever held auditions again for the Wicked Witch of the West, Becky would win. If a teacher strangled Becky in front of the entire student body at high noon, as long as there was one teacher on the jury, they'd never vote to convict. If there was a school rule she hadn't broken, I didn't know about it. Her mom is president of the school board. This explains a great deal.

The teachers hate Mrs. Twitchell almost as much as they hate Becky. As a freshman, Becky had complained to her mom about one first-year math teacher. Becky had made the class a total hell, and her mom had made so much trouble with the administration that the teacher had simply quit—and she had the makings of a good teacher. Rumor had it that if you got hold of Mr. Twitchell, you might see some chagrin in his daughter for a day or two. I'd never seen evidence of this.

The kid mouths off, talks back, hums, whistles, mumbles under her breath, or a combination of the above, in all classes. A large portion of the faculty believes Becky's behind every evil perpetrated in the school, from break-ins to broken windows. If kids were rebellious, it was Becky's fault for encouraging them. If there was cigarette smoke in the girls' john, they were sure it was Becky. If anti-teacher hate graffiti appeared painted on the school walls, Becky got blamed. The rare times Becky'd been caught, Mom had stepped in. Becky would return to school the next day with a shit-eating grin. Whatever political pressure occurred, Becky never served a minute of suspension or detention. She always won. She frightened many of the teachers. The only one of us who'd defied her this year found his tires slashed in the parking lot that afternoon.

I'd hated her last year as a junior. I'd felt her watching me in class, her mind whirling and calculating. I know, I know. As a teacher, you're supposed to care and be impartial. Every teacher I remember as a kid had favorites. Every teacher I knew on the faculty at Grover Cleveland High School had favorites. Face it, some kids are assholes. Some are great to know. Most teachers try to be fair. I've never changed a grade no matter how intensely I liked or disliked a kid.

"How do you get along with Becky?" I asked.

"She's Paul's girlfriend. What's to get along with? I try to stay out of her way. All the guys do. She's vicious."

Almost casually, I asked, "Did you know Susan was pregnant?"

His openmouthed surprise clicked in my mind as genuine. "She couldn't be," he said. "We always, I mean, I used, you know, protection." He told me the story of how after they'd dated awhile, Mrs. Warren had made Susan go to a family-planning clinic. She wouldn't talk to Susan about sex or being pregnant, but she made her go. Somehow, her mom had figured out about them. The clinic made Susan take Jeff along for a visit. After this explanation, tears rimmed his eyes, but he didn't cry. He said, "I thought she loved me."

I told him about condoms not being 100 percent sure, but he remained adamant. It wasn't him.

I switched to asking him how he got along with his mom and dad. Mom was a shrug and an "Okay, I guess." Much as I liked Mrs. Trask, I imagine she could be a bitch to live with. Mr. Trask was a sneer and an "I hate the bastard." He saw his dad very rarely. Last summer had been an experiment because he'd had a fight with his mom. Annoying as life with his mom had been, the months with his dad were worse.

I got the names of the other kids at the party. I'd want to talk to them the next day. We talked for a while longer, but he could give no indication of who might have wanted to hurt Susan, where she might have gone, or who she might have been with.

His last plea was for me to please help him, and a powerful reiteration of his innocence.

I told him it looked bleak but that I would do everything I could for him.

When I returned to the front desk, Mr. Trask and the group of kids had left.

I talked with Frank briefly. The last thing he said was, "If you believe Jeff is innocent, then obviously somebody else did it. A good place to start is with the other kids at the party. My cop instincts tell me something is up with them. I've never met such a closed-mouth group. I wanted to find out some basic information about the party. I couldn't get more than one or two words out of them. You're good at getting teenagers to open up to you. I'd appreciate it if you'd talk to them. See if you can find anything out.

I told him I'd give it a try.

Mrs. Trask drove me home. I assured her that I'd help Jeff. When she stopped to let me out, she reached over and gave me an awkward hug. I told her I would talk to her the next day.

I strolled between icy patches to the mailbox at the edge of the road. I could see Scott's car up the driveway fifty feet, next to the house.

Moonlight reflected off the windows of a car parked a hundred yards past my place. Cold night for kids to be out necking, I thought. The car's lights flicked on. I pulled open the mailbox: bills and junk mail. The car moved forward. Our arrival probably scared them off. Kids like to use the unlighted roads around my place for trysting. As long as they don't leave beer cans, used condoms, and other signs of teenage activity, I don't care. Usually, they drive past my place to the dimmer shadows of the cul de sac formed by the intersection with Interstate 80, a mile farther down my road.

The car shot forward. I eased a little farther off the pavement toward the mailbox. The car lights came straight at me and didn't slow down. I turned to dive for the ditch at the side of the road. My feet caught on an icy patch; I slipped, fell, scrambled to move. The oncoming lights blinded me for an instant. On hands and knees, I lurched toward the ditch. I couldn't get a grip because of the ice.

◣ 2 ◢

Horn blaring, engine roaring, the car flew by me. I'm still not sure how it missed. I got up, brushed myself off, and swore at the goddamn teenagers. The red taillights bobbed in the distance. I saw the car turn onto 183rd Street and race toward LaGrange Road. By the time I got in the house, found Scott's keys, and gave chase, it would have been too late.

Except for a couple scrapes on my hands, I wasn't hurt. The incident shook me a little. It had to be an innocent accident, I thought, hoped. A couple kids surprised necking or drinking beer, getting a little revenge. I tried to shrug it off. But the driver had long blond hair, and for an instant, although I couldn't testify to it, I thought it might have been Becky Twitchell. As I walked up the driveway, I decided I was paranoid.

I live in a farmhouse in the middle of one of the last cornfields in southwestern Cook County. The subdivisions creep closer every year. Soon I'll want to sell. I like the quiet. I own the house and two acres around it. The fields belong to a farmer I've seen only at a distance as he works the land.

Faint tapping sounds led me to the top of the basement steps. A variety of large and small engine parts lay scattered on the carpeted stairs. The taps became bangs as I maneuvered my way to the bottom of the steps. I found Scott visible from the waist down, under the washing machine.

I sat on the workout bench. My basement contains a furnace, a washer and dryer, two sets of weights, and a sump pump— all of which sit surrounded by four unadorned cinder-block walls. We need most of the room for our workouts. I heard a bang, a clatter, and a satisfied grunt. He can fix anything. I've known him to take machines declared terminally ill by a team of certified mechanics, place his hands over them, and the damn things heal. Until Eric Trask, Scott always worked on my cars.

A hand with a rust-encrusted jumble of metal, followed by a grime-shrouded arm, emerged from beneath the machine. "Take this, please," he said.

"I didn't know you heard me." I grabbed the thing and placed it on a pile of newspapers. "Anything else I can do?"

He gave me a muffled no. I retreated to the stairs.

"Got your message on the machine," he said.

"Good. I had to accompany Mrs. Trask to the police station." Several hammer bangs clanged out. "Eric stealing cars again?"

"No, Jeff, the younger brother, this time. They think he mur-dered his girlfriend."

He stuck his head out from under the washer. Dirty smudges covered his blond hair and half his forehead. "Murdered?"

"That's what the cops think." I told him the story while he worked. He grunted in appropriate places. On occasion, his left hand would reach out to the panful of tools, select one, and snake back under the machine. I could never figure out how he could get the exact right tool only by touch. While I talked, I admired the way his tight faded jeans clung to the contours of his body.

The loudest bangs of all came as I finished my story. A half-minute pause, then: "Shit, this thing is so fucked up. Why don't you let me buy you a new one?"

"I like that one. I'm used to it." At the start of our relationship nine years ago, he'd offered to buy me everything from cars to new homes. My pride then and now won't let me accept such things. On electronic gadgets I'd always wanted, like state-of-the-art computers, printers, and copiers, my pride loosened its grip.

"I've got another hour under here," he said. "Let's talk about the rest of this upstairs."

I thought about sitting and watching him work. One of our sexiest moments had been the time we made love on the floor of the garage underneath the jacked-up car. He'd been fixing the muffler, with me helping him. The grease, dirt, and slight danger added zest to the occasion.

I had another idea.

An hour later, he clumped up the basement stairs and walked into the kitchen. "Something smells good," he said. He stood next to me at the sink, washing the grease off his hands and arms. He eyed the stacks of dishes and pans strewn across all the counter space.

"How was your luncheon?" I asked.

"Pretty good, I guess. The food was nearly edible. The kid who got the M.V.P. award was so drunk, he couldn't stand up to accept the trophy. His coach had to rescue the situation. Embarrassed the kid's parents. The people who ran the banquet were nice."

As one of the highest-paid pitchers in the Major Leagues, Scott is in great demand as a speaker. He hurled two no-hitters in the World Series a couple years ago. At six four, he's an inch taller than I am. We work out together as often as possible, sometimes with the old weights downstairs, or in his Lake Shore Drive penthouse with its state-of-the-art equipment.

He wiped his hands on a dish towel and gave me a hug. He smelled of sweat and grease. I inhaled deeply. He reached around me and lifted the cover from a plate of freshly baked cookies. "White chocolate chip with macadamia nuts, my favorite." He nuzzled my ear. "What's the occasion?"

I rarely cook. Only my breakfasts are passable. It's hard to ruin toast. My cookies and cakes are edible. Generally, I try not to inflict my cooking on anyone. I avoid forcing foods into shapes God never intended. Besides, I'm not very good at it. Neither is Scott, although he does make an occasional holiday feast that is fabulous.

"This is a thank-you for fixing the washer, and a bribe to keep you from harassing me about not getting a new one, and for not finishing my Christmas shopping, and for not buying a new car."

"You didn't even call any dealers, did you?"

"I had to go with Mrs. Trask."

We sat at the kitchen table. I put a plate of cookies in front of him. I tried to avoid the shrewd look in his blue eyes.

"Do you want beer, milk, pop?" I asked.

"Milk."

I reached over to the refrigerator, grabbed the carton, poured him some, set it in front of him, and rested my elbows on the table.

"Did you at least talk to Eric about when the car might be done?"

They'd had to tow my car from the parking lot at school last week. My eight-year-old Chevette began to internally hemorrhage about a half mile from school. Even I, mechanical klutz that I am, knew that if this wasn't the car's death throes, it was a sign that a terminal illness had set in. Eric had said he wouldn't be able to finish it until early this week.

"No time to call," I said around a mouthful of cookie.

"Your mom called. You forgot to call her."

"Shit." I'd promised to make final Christmas plans with her today.

"She and I took care of next week's schedule."

I thanked him and promised to phone her later.

"And you didn't call about new cars?" Scott reiterated.

I ate a bite of cookie and tried to look innocent. He's right. I put everything off, or at least unpleasant shit. Although truly important things I never put off, as he'd see when he got his Christmas present. Also, I have gotten better over the years. It's not as if I can't afford a car. Maybe a nice sporty little thing with high gas mileage. I don't trust the Arabs and I want my new car to get more than fifty miles to the gallon, but I hate car shopping. He and I have argued about it before. The last time I bought a car, I walked on to the lot, found the cheapest one they had with the highest gas mileage, and told the salesman, "I want that one."

Scott wants me to dicker and deal and beat the salesman at his own game. I just want to get the hell out and be done with the bullshit. He nags me about it. Yes, I know my old Chevette is falling apart. I know I'll need another new transmission soon. I know I need new tires. I know it probably won't last the winter.

"I won't have time this week, but I promise I'll go."

"Before the end of the century?" he asked.

I gave him a dirty look.

"You don't need a car that could leave you stranded in weather like this. It's ten below out there right now. Frozen lover is not my idea of a wintertime treat."

I leveled my best teacher stare at him, guaranteed to freeze kids in seconds. "I told you I'd do it," I said.

We munched cookies and drank milk for a few minutes. Finally, I said, "I'm sorry. I'll take care of everything over vacation. I promise."

He grumbled around a bit of cookie, swallowed, and gave me one of his golden smiles. We returned to Jeff's arrest and my agreeing to help him.

For years, I've taught the slowest of the slow kids—usually seniors, sometimes sophomores. Their problems have been myriad and profound. I've testified at court hearings to remove kids from their abusive parents. I've gotten kids into drug and alcohol rehab programs. I've spent hours in the waiting rooms of abortion clinics. Sometimes it's worked out and the kids have turned their lives around and gone on to become productive adults; and some are in prison—arrested again after the best efforts of every concerned adult they know. A few are addicts, lost to themselves and society. Sometimes the frustrations get to me. I used to take them out on Scott. He doesn't put up with that kind of shit from me. He does worry because he knows what these things take out of me.

He frowned concernedly as I talked, then said, "You sure this is something you want to be a part of?"

"Definitely. I've known the family for years. I know most of the kids involved. Mrs. Trask has no one else to turn to. I think I can help."

"Okay. You know your limits, and I'll be there with you."

He finished the plate of cookies while I cleaned the kitchen. When I took his empty glass from the table, he chose that moment to remind me about the car. I scowled at him. "If you mention that again, young man, there'll be no sex for you for a week."

He grabbed me and pulled me onto his lap. "This is ridiculous," I said. His eyes gleamed impishly.

"Don't," I warned, but it was too late. He knows I'm ticklish in only one place—a spot not normally touched in casual contact. His hand roved down my chest.

As I finished cleaning, he sat perched on the clean countertop. He snapped his fingers. "I forgot. You had a message on the machine. Neil Spirakos is in the hospital."

I raised an eyebrow. "He finally had liposuction?"

"No. Serious, I guess. He said he'd been mugged and for you to call him. He's at Northwestern Memorial."

Neil's one of the reigning queens in the gay community in Chicago, and my best friend in the city. Too late to call tonight; I'd phone him tomorrow.

In bed, Scott said, "I'll be talking to your brother Glen tomorrow. We're set for his place Christmas Eve?"

"Yeah." Scott reads "The Night Before Christmas" and a million other stories to the youngest ones every year on Christmas Eve.

"Did your parents call?" I asked.

He shook his head no.

Scott had told his parents he was gay during his yearly visit after the baseball season. His parents are backcountry Alabama born-again Baptists. Their little boy sleeping with a man was too much for them. He'd had to cut short his visit because of their outrage and hurt.

My family, on the other hand, is nuts about him. We spend most holidays with them. My father and brothers get puffed up with pride having a star baseball player in the house. My nieces and nephews love him. Last Christmas, he spent hours rolling around outside in the snow with them. At least once each visit, my mother and sister corner me in the kitchen to tell me how wonderful he is and then urge me to accept his offers of us living together. One day, I'll accept their advice.

This year, he decided it was time I met his parents. He'd gone to prepare the way. Instead, he'd met rejection. This wasn't unusual, but it's tough to cope with. He'd hoped for a good response from his sister. They've been real close since they were kids. No such luck. I told him to give them more time.

I snuggled closer to his warmth and felt the first stirrings of drowsiness. He said, "I've been meaning to ask you something. Some of the guys on the team are throwing a New Year's Eve party. They're all my friends. It's going to be a small gathering, a couple guys and their wives."

"I can spend the evening listening to the Midnight Special New Year's Eve program on WFMT." I yawned.

"No. I'd like you to go with me." Doug Courtland, Scott's best friend on the team, had called to invite him. Numerous times, Scott has said that if he came out to anybody on the team, it would be Doug.

I came awake a bit more. "You sure you want me along?" For years, he'd kept his sexual orientation a huge secret. Fear of total shit hitting the fan if team management found out kept him closeted in the locker room. This would be a big step for him.

"I'm sure," he said as he draped an arm over my chest. I listened to his breathing. "It's not like I'm telling them anything. I'm not sure I'm ready for that. But I know I want you there. You can meet Jack Frampton and become his best friend." Frampton was the team's newest sensation. Still nineteen and voted rookie of the year, he bragged about how if he ever met a faggot, he'd beat the shit out of him. A couple times, Scott had barely contained himself from flattening the kid.

I caressed the hair on the arm that rested over me. "I'd be glad to go," I said. We lay in silence. I smelled faint whiffs of his after-shave, sweat, and toothpaste. As I drifted off to sleep, I thought about Jeff Trask and murder.

◣ 3 ◢

First thing next morning at school, I hunted for Kurt Campbell. He's coach of the football team and would know all the boys who'd been at the party. I wanted to learn as much as I could about each person involved. Kurt is also president of our teachers' union, and my best friend on the faculty.

In his classroom, I found him unraveling a red woolen scarf and unbuttoning his heavy parka. The temperature had plunged to fifteen below zero the night before. The weather forecasters had cheerfully predicted it would be twenty to twenty-five below tonight. I closed his classroom door, tossed my winter outer clothes onto a chair, and perched myself on a corner of his desk. Kurt wore dark brown dress pants, a beige sweater, a white shirt, and a striped brown and beige tie. He has a large nose, acne scars, and enormously broad, muscled shoulders. He claims his ugliness kept him from being trampled by all the girls when he was in high school. His wife, Beth, laughs uproariously whenever he says this. They'd dated since eighth grade.

"Damn, it's cold," he said. He rubbed his hands together for warmth. He eased himself into the chair behind his desk and propped his feet on the top.

"This had better not be union business," he said. "I am

unioned out. If I get one more complaint from a teacher or administrator before Christmas, I will personally strangle them."

He's been president of the union for over a decade. He led us through our first strike five years ago. He talked me into becoming union representative and grievance chairman for my building three years ago. Part of the duties included membership on the negotiations team. I got the job because no one else wanted it. He was grateful. I understood his frustration in not wanting to deal with another bitch or moan. Until I became building rep, I'd listened half-bemusedly to his complaints about teachers. Now that I'd heard their inanities directly for a few years, I knew exactly what he meant. And he has far more patience with them than I.

Teachers complain about the stupidest stuff. People expect the union to act sort of like an Old Testament God, only tougher and meaner. Usually, they need the union to get them out of trouble that they've gotten themselves into. And they whine. One school of educational thought says that teachers get more like the kids the longer they've been teaching. It is true teachers take three vows when they get their certificates: poverty, dedication, and the right to bitch.

"Complaints mounting up?" I asked.

He grimaced. "Last night's may have done it. A teacher at one of the elementary schools wanted me to force the principal to change the evaluation he gave her. The teacher said it wasn't fair that she got a satisfactory instead of an excellent rating. She said he observed her the day she was having her period. A fistfight between two kids with bloody noses and with the principal observing your second-grade class is not good."

"Off day for her?"

"From what I understood, it was one of her good days."

"Ouch."

"She told me that she was tired of the union not doing enough for her. How we're not tough enough. The usual shit from an idiot."

"Speaking of idiots, I've got to see Pete Montini and George Windham today."

"You have my sympathy."

Pete is head coach and George is his assistant on the basketball team. For a few years, they've shared minor duties on the football program. They know the boys more than most other teachers and at least as well as Kurt. They are also the biggest assholes in the school.

Kurt asked, "What do you need to see them about?"

I explained to him about Jeff, last night, and the kids at the party.

I also explained about Mrs. Trask. He liked her, too. Most teachers who'd talked to her did.

He gave me his opinion of the kids involved. Becky he knew only by reputation. "As for Susan, I find it hard to believe she had a boyfriend. I had her for algebra two years ago. I remember her as a loner. I never saw her exchange a word with a classmate." Doris Bradford he didn't know. Same for Eric Task. On Paul Conlan; "You couldn't ask for a better kid. I coached him for four years of football. Did what you asked. Smart. Willing to give of himself for the team. And the kid could play. Excellent chance of a scholarship to a good school. He's an even better basketball player."

Kurt found Jeff funny, liked him and his loony sense of humor. The boy worked hard on the football field.

"Even with his muscles, I thought he was kind of tall and thin to be a middle linebacker," I said.

"He's got that willingness to throw himself at an opponent with almost insane abandon. I've seen him go through an opponent with unbelievable mercilessness. He's also got a temper. Angry enough, I've seen him flatten boys who outweigh him by a hundred pounds."

"Enough temper to kill somebody?"

"I don't know. Possible. I'd hope not."

Roger Daniels, the last one he had in class, Kurt said was a

31

good football player—a hulking kid almost as wide as he was tall. I'd had Roger in class as a freshman. Then, he'd been the class clown—a red-haired dynamo who looked like he could take on the world. Kurt confirmed this as currently correct.

Kurt finished: "I only coached Roger, but he didn't strike me as overly bright. The only real intelligent one of the bunch was Conlan. Sorry I can't help you more. Both Montini and Windham had a lot of these kids in class as well as coaching them on the basketball team. I don't envy you talking to them."

Before I left, we set a tentative Friday-night date for a Christmas visit from Scott and me and for me to pick up more negotiations material.

At noon, I went to talk to Pete Montini. I found him in his classroom near the gym. Pete is tall, broad, and bald. He has the well-muscled body of a recently in-shape heavyweight wrestler. Rumor says he has the worst breath among any of the faculty. Behind his back, the kids call him "Dragon Mouth." He also is known for his prodigious ability to consume candy bars. His muscles look a few ounces away from a great deal of fat, with a heart attack soon to follow. The head basketball coach, he also teaches several American government classes.

Pete is in his mid-forties—a man soured on kids and teaching but with no place else to go. He is the living vision of the cliché "Those who can, do; those who can't, teach." He'd wanted to be a pro football player, had the height and weight to play, but, for reasons unknown to me, had never made it. Ten years ago, he'd picked up a kid and thrown him down the school's front stairs. He barely escaped an assault charge. They'd suspended him for thirty days without pay. He came back a chastened and frightened man.

When I walked into his room, he and Paul Conlan abruptly stopped talking. I apologized for interrupting and turned to leave. Pete stopped me. He said it was all right—the boy was just leaving.

As he walked out, I asked Paul whether I could see him after school to discuss Jeff and Sunday's party. He gave the coach a fearful look. I saw Pete give him a brief nod of permission. I wondered what the connection was there. The kid left.

"He looks worried," I said.

"Grades. Eligibility. He wants me to talk to one of his teachers."

Paul Conlan worried about grades? I guessed it was possible. Pete eased into a broken-down swivel chair and invited me to sit. I found a bare spot on his desk and did so. Chicago Bears posters covered the walls. The Gale Sayers and Dick Butkus ones dated back to before the Bears won the Super Bowl. Kids' shouts seeped into the classroom from the gym next door. Pete pulled out a bottom desk drawer and rested his feet on it. He leaned back in his chair, picked up a tennis racket from the top of his desk, and twirled it in sporadic jerks.

I gave my little spiel about helping Jeff and asked for anything he could tell me about the kids at the party.

He said, "I've coached Jeff for three years. He'd never hurt her. They were in love." The racket twirled. "Although," he said slowly, "Jeff's got quite a temper. I can see him going out of control." He told me about a basketball game early in December. A ref had called Jeff for a foul. Montini thought it was a bum call, but Jeff had gone nuts. Before Montini could bench him, Jeff had two technical fouls called against him. Then the kid threw a chair and the ref tossed him out of the game.

The information I had so far didn't look good for Jeff. It confirmed that he had a violent temper. I'd seen it myself the night before with his dad. I asked about the other kids.

He said, "First, I've got to add a couple nice things about Jeff. He's easy to coach. Always does what I tell him. A good athlete. Not great. He's never going to be in the pros, but he'd be a starter on most high school teams." He added that Mr. Trask expected Jeff to play in the pros. The father pushed his son really hard for success, but Montini didn't understand it. Mr. Trask wouldn't be the first dad disappointed over a son's career.

Jeff played a decent game of basketball but was better at football. His emotion worked for him there.

"I don't want you to get the impression I'm down on Jeff or anything. I like the kid. Why, one time, he even stayed overnight at my house."

"How'd that happen?"

"I've had kids stay overnight a few times. Mostly if they don't have anywhere to go, usually had a big fight with their parents. Mostly guys from the team. It's no big deal."

He told the story about Jeff between tosses and twirls of the tennis racket. After the last home football game in October, Montini had walked out to his car. Jeff and his dad had been standing nose to nose in the middle of the parking lot, screaming at each other. The argument centered around what Mr. Trask thought Jeff should have done in the game. The old man pointed out every fault the boy had, including the way he sat on the bench. His dad stormed off. Montini'd thought father and son had similar tempers. Jeff had planned to stay at his dad's that night. He told Montini that he and his dad didn't get along, even though they didn't see each other that much. The boy didn't want to hassle with his mom. It was after eleven, so Montini let him stay over at his place.

"I never met the father before last night," I said.

"The man is a son of a bitch. When he comes to the games, he screams at his boy in front of everybody. The kid has a hard time concentrating on the game with his damn dad bellowing at him."

I'd known that type of parent—living through the sports achievements of their kids. I'd seen them at games, torturing their sons and daughters with bellowed advice while the poor kids tried to master a few skills their coach had taught them. The idiot parents expected all-pro play from high school kids. Once I'd seen a parent get his comeuppance. At a basketball game in front of four thousand people, a kid turned to his dad, who from ten rows up in the bleachers had been screaming at his son. The boy stood still while the rest of the players ran down the court. Then he came to the edge of the stands, looked up to where his dad sat, pointed at his dad, and yelled, "Shut up, you stupid motherfucker." The crowd around the father cheered the son. Instead of suspending him for the season, they should have given the kid a medal. I appreciated the impulse and wished I could see it more often. My parents came to most of my games in high school, and once or twice in college. My dad got excited sometimes, but he never embarrassed me in front of packed bleachers—an important consideration for a teenager.

Montini twirled the tennis racket in his left hand, then tossed it to his right. "Now your Susan Warren, she got friends because she dated Jeff. Unfortunately, they weren't the greatest girls. Susan was a follower. She was closest to Conlan's girl, Becky Twitchell."

He hated Becky Twitchell. He had her in class two years ago. He hadn't dared turn his back on the class the whole semester. He was sure she was the one behind the vandalism in the boys' locker room. Every football and basketball had been slashed to ribbons, along with several thousand dollars' damage to the room itself. "It all happened after I gave her an F for the first quarter. I'm sure it was that bitch."

"Why would a guy go out with a creep like Becky?" I asked.

"Why not? She's hot-looking. If she was older, I'd be interested. Or maybe she's easy." He gave me a leer, then continued. "She's pretty and a cheerleader. Susan, being a quiet kid, would fall in with Becky pretty easily. Susan was a nice kid. Sometimes she would wait for Jeff after practice. It was kind of cute. They were pretty serious about each other." He didn't know of any problems they might have been having.

Pete didn't know Roger and Doris. Paul, of course, was God. "The kid has everything. He's going places. He's got half the recruiters in the country breathing down his neck. He's good-natured, polite, cooperative, mature, a leader. I can't say enough good things about him. We'd have a state-championship team if I had only one more kid half as good as he is."

Pete knew of no one who might have a motive for killing Susan.

The odd thing I thought about as I left the room was that Pete Montini had been friendly and more cooperative than I'd ever dreamed. I'd known him for twelve years and every single conversation with him until then had contained at least one complaint, plus sarcasm and nasty digs. As building rep, I'd dealt with all the grievances he'd filed with the union. He didn't particularly like me, I didn't think. I had a tendency to tell him when his complaints were silly bullshit. I guess a good union representative is supposed to smile quietly and go along with whatever inanities the complainer brings. Somehow, I can't go along with that. He hasn't complained about the quality of rep-resentation I've given him. I shrugged it off for the moment. Maybe murder was enough to make him a little cooperative.

In the hallway outside my classroom, I ran into Meg Swarthmore. She grasped my elbow and dragged me into my classroom. "I must talk to Detective Inspector Mason," she said.

I like Meg. We've been friends for years. She's the school librarian—a tiny woman, not over five feet tall, plump in a grandmotherly way. She's in her sixties and could have retired years ago.

Meg's the ultimate clearinghouse for all school gossip. She hears everything. If there were secrets to be known, Meg would have them to tell. She has one cardinal rule: Never reveal a source.

I told her what'd happened so far.

When I finished, she said, "A hell of a mess. I'm glad you're going to help. It might be the only chance that boy has."

"You're exaggerating, Meg." I reddened under her praise.

"Don't give me that humble bullshit. You can hide how much

you do for these kids from lots of people around here, but not from me, and not from your friends like Kurt. We know you too well."

I told her my suspicions about how friendly Montini had been and about my projected talk with Windham.

She harrumphed sarcastically. "The two of them are a waste of good breathable atmosphere. Talking to them is less than useless. They're a couple of losers. I don't see why they're teachers. They hate kids. I've heard them say so in the lounge. The two of them are both horny, nuts, and desperate. I know for a fact they've both cheated on their wives."

"Come on, Meg."

"You doubt my veracity?"

"Well, no."

"Good thing. If you ask me, either one of those two is as likely to be the killer as Jeff Trask."

"Why?"

"They're a couple of worn-out ex-jocks who haven't gotten beyond the last touchdown they scored in high school. Do you know where they were at the time of the killing?"

"No. But you're being prejudiced."

She gave me a wicked grin. "You betcha. You want the low-down on Pete?" I nodded. "This first is opinion. He'd sell his grandmother and his soul for a winning team. He pressures kids on his teams unmercifully. He has no concept of what it does to the kids emotionally. The boys on the team, however, like him in general. No major fights among the faculty. Congenial head of the department. Not the brightest."

"How about George Windham?"

"Mr. Mystery of the faculty. Been here five years, and as sneaky as they come."

"You mean he's escaped your usually omnipotent grapevine."

She nodded. "Yeah. That doesn't happen often, and that makes me very suspicious. Around here, if I don't know it, then it shouldn't be there to tell. Sarah, his wife, worked in the English department years ago. She wasn't around long enough for me to find out anything. But I've got a hunch about George. Drugs and kids. Don't ask me more now. I've had suspicions for a long time. I'll come back with something solid as soon as I can."

She got up to leave but turned back at the door. "Everything's set for our annual brunch, Saturday."

Every year, Scott and I spend the first Saturday of my Christmas vacation at Meg's. We exchange presents and share a two-hour lunch.

I have an after-school tutoring group every day except Fridays. After they left, I hurried to the gym to talk to George Windham. I found him in the hall outside the gym, clad in sweat-drenched maroon gym shorts and a T-shirt carefully ripped to show athletic muscles. He held a basketball in one hand. He breathed deeply. The lopsided grin that greeted me showed his perfect teeth and a youthful smile, indication of the goofy good humor he showed on numerous occasions. Over the years, he'd lost his southern Illinois twang. George could be friendly, cheerful, and happy-go-lucky. He could also be one of the greatest bitches in the teachers' lounge. His imitation of the administrators in the district were legendary, and more than once brought me to tears of laughter. He also said some of the dumbest things. On occasion, I thought his whole dumb routine was more an act than real. How he could have an even partly sunny disposition with six kids at home I couldn't imagine. He worked construction jobs in the summer and other odd jobs at night to help make ends meet.

George had been officially reprimanded by the administration five times—all since he had gotten tenure. Twice he'd been caught walking out of teachers' institutes at noon and not returning. He hadn't mentioned to me when he came crying for help the second time that there'd been a distinct odor of marijuana in his car when the administrator had caught him at the edge of the parking lot. I found that out through the school gossip vine.

Once, he'd kept a kid after school until eight at night. The kid's frantic parents finally located him. Once, he'd got into a shouting match with one of the administrators in front of an auditorium filled with kids. Another time, he'd failed to complete all the paperwork in his homeroom's folders at the end of the school year. He'd declared that paperwork was beneath him and chose not to do it.

I managed to convince him to break his habit of sneaking in late every day, before he got caught.

George always had a pleasant tease ready for me as a greeting, usually as a preface to a new problem or complaint. I think he viewed me as a necessary curmudgeon who'd gotten him out of numerous tight scrapes with the administration. In all the years and with all the dumb things he's done, they still give him a paycheck. Maybe it's his considerable good looks.

"I've got to stop playing one-on-one with these kids," he panted. "I'm not getting any younger."

"I bet they like it. Did you win?"

"Of course; it wouldn't do for a coach to lose to a kid."

I gave my spiel about Jeff. He glanced in the gym door, called a kid over, and told him to tell Mr. Montini he'd be right back.

We eased into a nearby classroom. The first thing he said was, "My guess is some teenage murderer's on the loose, like in a teenage horror movie. I can think of a whole list of kids I'd like him to start with. I'd even help with some of them."

When he got serious, he started with Roger Daniels. He was a decent kid. On the team bus, Roger led the chants and songs. He could be a real spark plug on the team. They found him tough to motivate because he wanted to goof around too much. If they were lucky during a game, an opponent would make him mad. Then Roger could devastate the other team on offense or defense.

Another kid with a temper problem.

Eric Trask, when he'd worked with him two years ago, had been too dumb to be a real asset on the basketball team, but he was too tall to be cut. "He still hangs around with some of the guys," he said. "They seem to like him. Susan and Doris never said much in class and I only had them one semester, so I don't really know them. Even with the kids on the team, you've got to remember, I don't know them all that well. I'm only an assistant coach. I'm not in love with these kids the way Montini is."

"I heard your name mentioned concerning kids and drugs," I said. "I'm not accusing, just checking out everything."

His face turned beet red under his light blond hair. "Who told?" he asked.

"It's true?"

He gave a disgusted sigh. He walked to the windows and turned to face me. The December gloom gathered behind him. "You ever go home to a houseful of squalling kids and a nagging wife? I swear that woman keeps a chart of all my movements. She remembers everything: how long it takes to get home from work; what time practices end. She has it down to the minute. Sometimes I need something to calm me down so I can face all that. I mean the goddamn house is one vast dirty diaper. Half-dressed kids run around screaming and yelling. I'm only twenty-eight and I feel like ninety-eight. I've got to have some diversion. And don't tell me you haven't at least tried a little dope, not after having been a Marine in Vietnam."

I ignored his comment and said, "Alcohol, I could maybe understand, but drugs and kids?"

"That was an accident. It only happened a couple times. My supplier from Carbondale used to get me stuff sent up here. He got busted a few months back. I was desperate. Finally, an old buddy put me in touch with some people here. A couple turned out to be connected with Grover Cleveland. Once or twice, it was just easier to pick the stuff up from the kids, and some of them happened to be current students."

"George, that's stupid," I said. "They could turn on you at some point. You could lose your job, career, go to jail. Buying drugs from kids is dumb."

"I've got my old supplier back," he assured me. His boyish smile lit his face. "He got paroled two weeks ago. I'm safe."

I gave him a disgusted look, then asked, "What about the other kids?"

"Paul Conlan is great. Tops in school, tops on the basketball court. Always polite. Self-assured. Going places.

"Now, Becky Twitchell is poison. I had her as a freshman. Caught a note she was trying to pass. I started to read it in front of the class. She screamed and got abusive. The note was more pornographic than anything I'd ever read, offering to perform specific lascivious acts for some boy."

Lots of teachers found reading notes out loud a useful tactic. I found it an intrusive waste of time. I took the notes and deposited them in the nearest trash can. What was the point of humiliating the kids? Probably, they've been passing notes since people first scrawled on stone tablets. There may be times to embarrass kids as an effective teaching tool, but I'm not aware of them. As an adult, I don't know anybody who enjoys being embarrassed, so I don't think kids do, either.

George continued: "Becky grabbed at the note. It ripped. She managed to get the part that contained her signature and most of the obscene stuff. Before I could get hold of it, she tore her part into a thousand pieces and pitched them out the third-floor window."

He shrugged ruefully, picked up a pencil, and tapped it on the desk. He explained that he'd bellowed at her for five minutes. She took it all with a sneer on her face. When he got done, all she said was, "Don't ever try that again, you son of a bitch." Right in front of the whole class, she'd said this. He'd sent her to the office. He said, "You know how they are with most kids, but especially board-member kids. She got a hug and a 'Don't do it again, dear.'"

"That the end of it?"

"No. The next morning, I went out to start my car. Radiator fluid covered the driveway. Later, the mechanic told me somebody deliberately had punched holes in it. Cost me five hundred and fifty dollars to get it repaired."

"And you couldn't prove who did it?"

"Of course not. But Becky wore her shit-eating grin for a week in my class. I'm sure it was her. You hear about her taking revenge on teachers."

Jeff was one of the best dumb kids he'd ever had on the team. Sometimes, you could see him on the court thinking about what they'd taught him and what he was supposed to do next. Unfortunately, by that time, the play had passed him by. But you knew he wanted to do it right. With his height and natural ability, they couldn't keep him off the team.

That was all he could tell me. He knew nothing of the kids' activities that Sunday.

I wanted to talk to Paul Conlan, but it was only five and practice wouldn't be over for a half hour. I decided to try the office. I could look up the files on these kids and see whether they revealed anything in any of their pasts that might be helpful. I found Georgette Constantine, the school's beloved secretary, in the office. A major ditz, always befuddled, but willing to bend over backward to help you—in her limited way.

As I walked in, she slapped the intercom machine twice. "Please work," she whispered at it. An electronic squawk followed by a pleasing hum brought a smile to her face. I'd hate to have to rely on the system to call for help if crazed students or parents attacked me while in a classroom.

I cleared my throat. She noticed me and fluttered over. "Mr. Mason, you're here late."

I explained what I was after.

"The police did the same thing earlier. I made them put everything back exactly where they found it."

"Is Mrs. Blackburn in?" I asked.

Carolyn Blackburn was our new principal. A gray-haired woman in her mid-fifties, she'd fought with tact and efficiency to turn around a floundering school. She patrolled the halls personally, insisting on discipline and order. She made the usual promises new principals do: that she wanted to be a true part of the education process; that she'd try to be in our classrooms not to observe or be threatening but so that we could all sit down together to make education a better experience for the children. I'd heard that bullshit from every administrator for whom I'd ever worked. A few of the newer teachers get all upset because they feel threatened when an administrator comes to observe them. We veterans know better. Administrators try it for a month, then the trivia, paperwork, ass kissing, and other vital functions of a school principal overwhelm them and we're left alone. That's the way it worked out with Blackburn. I guess she isn't a bad person. I'd spoken to her on a number of occasions. I trusted her as much as you can trust any administrator.

I told her briefly about the murder and the kids involved, especially Becky Twitchell. Late for a meeting, she didn't have time to talk but promised to get back to me the next day with information on Becky.

I made a painstaking search of each child's file from kindergarten to high school. I found records of bumps and bruises and standarized test scores and registration forms and grades, but not a thing to indicate who might be involved in a murder. Just after 5:45, I walked to the gym to talk to Paul Conlan. When I looked in the door, the basketball court was dark, practice obviously over. I debated going to the locker room but gave it up. I'd catch him tomorrow.

Walking down the hall toward the exit to the parking lot, I

heard a door slam. I turned a corner. Gray lockers, interrupted by a six-foot trophy case on one side, lined the hallway. Only half the lights were still on at this hour. The winter dark seeped through the glass doors at the end of the hall.

A dim figure loomed at the end of the hall.

4

Paul and I stood alone in the dim hallway. Under his Grover Cleveland High School letterman's jacket, he wore a bulky knit sweater that had a row of reindeer prancing merrily from shoulder to shoulder. He wore tight black pants and gleaming white high-top basketball shoes.

"I came back to get my gym bag." He held up the item mentioned. His soft deep voice thrummed through the corridor. He stood at least six foot five and weighed 220 pounds. I remember seeing Paul as a skinny six-foot freshman. He spent that year quietly and meekly. Then his voice had stopped squeaking, he'd grown five inches, gained seventy pounds, and now as a senior was president of the class and co-captain of the football team. Now boys flocked around him and girls swooned. I couldn't figure out what a kid with so much going for him saw in Becky Twitchell.

In the dimly lit hallway, he avoided making eye contact. I explained about helping Jeff. "Anything you can tell me about Sunday's party might help," I said.

He shifted his books from his right hand to his left. He whispered, "I can't."

"You're a friend of his. Don't you want to help him?"

"Yeah." He returned his books to his right hand, leaned one

elbow on the trophy case, and rubbed his face with his other hand.

"Did you talk to the police?"

He nodded.

"Something go wrong with them?"

"Yeah. No." He peered at me, looked away.

I pondered on how to break through his teenage reticence. Obviously, something was wrong. I let the silence build.

"Man, this is too much." He paused. Silence ticked away. "Lots of the kids say you can be trusted. That you've helped some of the guys out of tough situations and didn't tell their parents."

I confirmed his statement with a nod.

Suddenly, he bashed the flat of his hand against the glass of the trophy case. "Everybody has to get off my back." He gave me an agonized look.

"Who's on your back?"

"My parents, Becky, Mr. Montini, the police, you. I didn't do anything. Jeff killed her." He gave me a horrified look. "Shit," he muttered. He swung his head from side to side. "This is too much."

I let a few moments of silence develop, then asked, "You didn't tell the police that you think he killed her?"

"I didn't lie."

"You didn't tell all?"

He nodded.

"Why do you think he killed her?"

"Jesus, I can't squeal on a friend." His knuckles on the hand clutching his books shone whitely. His shoulders hunched with tension.

I said, "I'm willing to listen. I'd like to help."

He gazed at me, turned his back to the wall, and slid down it until his ass rested on the tile floor. He spread his legs, slumped his rear a foot from the wall, closed his eyes, and softly set his books on the floor next to him. "Okay," he mumbled.

I sat down opposite him, our feet perhaps ten inches apart.

I felt the cold of the floor on my ass. Probably dirty. He sighed. The red of the exit sign made the side of his head toward the doors glow oddly.

"Tell me about Sunday's party."

He described an average teenage party, a little beer, and, under prodding from me he admitted, a few drugs. A few guys from the team and their girlfriends got together every Sunday. They went to his house to watch football games because his parents never bothered them, and he had the widest-screen television.

About Jeff and Susan, he was specific. "They had a big fight even before they left my house Sunday."

"What about?"

"It started because she wanted him to take her to a dance next week. He wouldn't go. Jeff got stubborn like he always does. Usually, he acts like a jerk, then agrees to go. She used to have to nag endlessly to get him to do anything. He didn't like to do stuff."

"I thought Susan was a quiet girl."

"Not this year. She wanted to do everything and go everywhere. Said she wanted to make her senior year count, make up for lost time."

"What did they actually say to each other that night?"

"We were all kind of teasing him. The girls, Becky especially, were after him. I was, too. I mean we were friends, teammates all these years, but he could be such a jerk."

He fiddled with the cover of his *American Government in Action* textbook, his fingernail working on a loose corner, drawing the cover picture away from the binding.

"So what happened?"

"Sunday, he acted jerkier than usual. He wouldn't say anything, just kept asking Susan to leave with him, way before everybody else wanted to go."

"How were they when they left?"

"Pissed. Susan especially. Jeff practically dragged her out. He was really mad. I could tell. People yelled, especially Becky, trying to get him to let Susan alone. But she left with him. I think maybe she didn't want to be the only girl at the party without a boyfriend."

"They were angry, but why would that make you think he killed her?"

"The stuff they yelled at each other."

"Like what?"

He gulped. "Like Susan dared Jeff to hit her. Said he couldn't talk without hitting her. Dumb stuff, but I think she meant it. When she said that to him, he swung at her, but he missed. He tried to swing again, but I grabbed him until he cooled down."

They'd walked to the car, still arguing—Susan shouting that she wasn't going to be a doormat; Jeff telling her to listen to him for once.

"You and Jeff were pretty good friends?"

"I was his best friend on the team, but I've got lots of friends. I think he only had a couple. He's a good player. We got along. He knows a lot about sports. We've gone to a few Bulls games together."

"What'd you think of Jeff and Susan's relationship before Sunday?"

"Okay, I guess. They had their little arguments, you know, but . . ." He shrugged.

"Why not tell all this to the police?"

"If the cops thought Jeff and Susan had a fight, they'd be more likely to think Jeff did it. You can't tell on your friends. I've never done it. If anybody ever told on me, I'd pound the crap out of them. Besides, who wants to be involved in a hassle like this?"

'What about Becky? How does she see all this?"

"You know, sometimes I don't understand her." He gave me a look of teenage wistfulness. I saw what he must have looked like as a three- or four-year-old gently puzzling over a butterfly emerging from a cocoon. He continued: "She was on the phone right away Sunday night, telling me we couldn't tell about the fight. She said we shouldn't rat on our friends. She said everybody would know if we cooperated with the police."

"That sounds stupid," I said.

"I guess." He looked sheepish. "I was kind of confused." He gave me a weak smile. "Nobody I know has ever been murdered." He shook his head. "But won't telling you all this make it worse for Jeff? I mean, all this is bad stuff. How will it help him?"

"I don't know yet. But I think the truth usually helps more than lies." I wasn't sure I bought that completely, but it was the correct teacherly thing to say for the moment. I thought for a minute.

"You didn't see either Jeff or Susan the rest of the night?"

"No."

"You and the coach today at noon—" I began.

He interrupted. "That was about the team and our next game."

"You going to be eligible?"

I got a confused look from him. "Why shouldn't I be? My lowest grade's a C in calculus."

I mumbled a disclaimer to him while considering the lie that either he, Montini, or both had told me.

"Were Becky and Susan good friends?" I asked.

"I guess. All those girls sort of hung out together. Best friends one day, catty bitches the next. Kind of typical girls." He paused. "Can I leave? I have to be home."

I let him go.

I'd called Scott from the school office, asking him to pick me up at six. His lone car sat in the parking lot as I walked out the door.

We stopped at my place, barely managed to keep from burning some leftovers, and ate them. Over dinner, I told Scott about George and drugs. Scott asked whether I was going to turn him in. I'd thought about it. However, George didn't do drugs on school grounds as far as I knew, and he didn't go to school doped up. I didn't see him as some mad-fiend addict mugging kids for their lunch money. After dinner, we drove to Mrs. Trask's. Events had moved too quickly the day before to talk with her as much as I'd wanted.

Mrs. Trask lived a mile north of the police station in the oldest section of River's Edge, off of 159th Street. The house stood on a slight rise, with a twenty-foot front yard and only a bare patch of dirt for a backyard. Snow had been meticulously shoveled from all the sidewalks and the driveway. I saw Eric's candy-apple-red Corvette in the driveway. I could check with him about my car before we left. Mrs. Trask met us at the front door. She was dressed in blue jeans and a black sweater, both of which bagged indecorously on her as usual. Distant hard-rock music indicated the presence of Eric somewhere in the house.

We passed through the living room, which contained countless mismatched knickknacks in ordered rows on the floor-to-ceiling shelves that covered three walls. Not a speck of dust sat on any of them. The paraphernalia ranged from cheap kids' dinosaurs, to pet Snoopys, to little men whose heads bobbed in the breeze. Few of them seemed to rise above the level of bargain-basement specials. A soundless television showed Vanna White twirling letters. We sat in the kitchen—no knickknacks here, but the pattern of neatness continued.

I introduced Scott. She vaguely recognized the name but made no comments. She probably wasn't up on sports. I asked for the latest on Jeff.

"Not much. The lawyer said he's still trying to get bail." She offered us beer as we sat at the kitchen table. She stood leaning her ample back end against the sink. "I'm not sure that lawyer knows what he's doing," she said. "I know it's not supposed to be like Judge Wapner's courtroom, but I just don't understand what the problem is. I know my boy didn't kill her. The police won't tell me anything. And when I try to talk to the lawyer on the phone, he's always in meetings. I have a right to know what's going on."

We commiserated on the cruelties of the system. I glanced around at the avocado-colored refrigerator, pale pink drapes, and gleaming white linoleum.

I explained what I'd done so far that day in trying to help Jeff.

She said, "It's hard for me to believe that any of them could do such a thing. I've known most of them since grade school, when I was a room mother. Susan was the first girl Jeff ever loved. When he was in eighth grade, he always seemed to take girls so serious, but he was shy. 'Course in these last couple years, he hasn't talked to me much. All teenagers are like that. But a mother knows when her boy's in love."

I asked about Jeff and Mr. Trask.

She went on a seven-minute tirade about the man I'd seen her pounding to a pulp the day before. She explained that he did everything to drive the children away from her. After she wound down about him, I got her back on the subject of the kids.

"Paul Conlan and Jeff have played together since kindergarten. They've had all the fights and scrapes two boys do. They used to be pretty equal in sports, but then Paul just shot past him. I hate those games. I don't understand what they're trying to do. I watch, but I'm hopeless. Jeff is a good athlete, so I encourage him. I try to get to as many of his games as I can."

Eric bounced into the room, saw us, and gave a breezy greeting. He only paused a second or two when I introduced Scott. His reaction was, "Wow, cool. The guys at the garage won't believe I met you." He stood at the open refrigerator, extracted a half gallon of milk, and, over his mother's protests, chugged a few gulps directly from the carton. He wore a heavy pea coat. On his way out, he told me he'd be sure to get to my car tomorrow. I managed to stop him long enough for him to agree to talk to me at school around four o'clock the next day. He told me he'd drive the car over if it was finished, then he left.

CHICAGO HEIGHTS PUBLIC LIBRARY

Mrs. Trask sighed. "They don't listen to me." She offered us another beer, but we declined. We moved to the living room. From the corner of a sagging couch, I observed the filled shelves. Amid the paraphernalia, I saw portraits of her kids. I recognized them as school photos in cheap frames. Mrs. Trask eased her bulk into an imitation leather chair and shook her head.

"I feel most sorry for that Paul Conlan," she said. "He's such a sad boy."

"He's popular, smart, and his dad's rich," I said.

"That don't mean nothing. He's a sad boy. My husband is a fool, but Paul's parents are worse. They have no idea what a good son they have."

She saw the doubt on my face. "No, he's not one of the ones likely for you ever to help. It's, well, it's . . ." She paused, then told about an incident six years ago. On a rainy summer night, Paul had walked to the Trask home. The boys had lost the baseball championship game that afternoon before it rained. All the parents had crammed into the stands—Paul's parents and Mr. Trask screaming at the boys, the coach, each other. Mrs. Trask was afraid there'd be a fight. Paul struck out every time he batted, which included the last out with the bases loaded. She finished, "Paul had been the star of the team all season. All they could do was scream his name."

Her beefy arms thumped the side of the chair. "This was before I divorced that son of a bitch. He was out that night with the boys buying an ice cream. Paul came to our house still in his baseball uniform, dirty streaks of tears on his face. He didn't say anything. We sat on the front porch. I held him as he cried. What kind of parents make a twelve-year-old that miserable? They've pressured those kids every minute for years with this sports junk." She shuddered. "I don't mean to insult you, Mr. Carpenter, you being a sports person and all, but really."

Scott told her that he understood. I know he did. We'd talked before about the pressure from coaches and parents. Mine had been okay, fortunately, but his dad had been among the worst of the ranters and ravers. One time, he'd beaten up Scott's Little League coach for what Scott's dad considered to be a wrong choice for his boy.

Mrs. Trask continued, "And poor Becky Twitchell." This I sat up for. Nobody had ever expressed even the slightest positive feeling for Becky and here was someone feeling sorry for her. "The girl is sick," Mrs. Trask said. That sounded more like everybody else. "I tried for years to keep her away from these boys. She's smarter and cleverer than me. I've tried and tried." She shook her head. "I guess I do hate her, although I know that's wrong. I'll have to go to confession about that, but it's true. When the boys told lies, lots of times it was to cover for Becky. If the kids were unhappy, it was because Becky got her way."

Roger she found funny. Doris was a delightfully helpful girl.

We talked a while longer, but we'd learned all we could from her. As we retrieved our coats from the hall closet, she said, "You're not the only teacher that cares at that school; that coach, Mr. Windham, called to talk to Eric. He told me how sorry he was about everything. It's nice to know people at the school care."

Maybe George did care, but I hadn't noticed anything in him besides selfish irresponsibility. And why talk to Eric? Maybe I'd find out tomorrow.

Before we left, I assured her I'd talk to the lawyer in the morning about bail for Jeff. As we stood at the door her eyes filled with tears. She took my hand. "You've got to help," she pleaded. "You're my boy's only hope."

I assured her as best I could.

The bitter cold driven by a twenty-mile-an-hour east wind tore through us as we hurried to the car. Rubbing gloved hands together as the car warmed up, I asked, "Have we got time to get to the hospital to see Neil before visiting hours close?"

"It's supposed to start snowing anytime, but yeah, we've probably got time," Scott said.

We took LaGrange Road to the Stevenson Expressway and drove to Northwestern Memorial Hospital. I'd called earlier in the day, but Neil'd been asleep. A quick visit would be enough. He's been a leading gay activist for years. We'd worked on several committees together in the early eighties to get the police to stop harassing gay bars and to get the Gay Rights Ordinance passed in Chicago and Illinois. Neil could have a vicious tongue. When I first introduced him to Scott, Neil used to condescend cruelly to him—Neil tended to look down on anyone who didn't have an advanced degree from a prestigious university. Today, they existed in an uneasy truce with each other.

By luck, we found a parking place on Chicago Avenue, in front of the National Guard Armory, about a block from the hospital. We made a short dash through the cold down Fairbanks and into the hospital a half hour before visiting hours ended. We found his room on the fourth floor, having left a gentle stir behind us when one of the nurses on duty recognized Scott.

We found Neil awake, alone, and bitchy as hell. "Salvation, take me away," he commanded when he saw us. "They're poisoning me." One leg lay in traction. He had a private room, of course. His wealth earned him that much.

I looked at the still uncleared remnants of dinner—swirls of muck awash between green lumps. "It's just hospital food," I offered.

He rolled his eyes. He complained for the better part of ten minutes about life, the world, the lack of cute male nurses, the harridans who did take care of him, the demeaning hospital gowns, the awful schedule, waking up too early.

"You can't be that badly hurt," I said.

This provoked an extensive listing of a variety of aches, pains, bumps, and bruises. Besides the leg, his only obvious wounds were nasty bruises deepening to ugly black eyes.

"What happened?" I asked.

He gave us each an angry look. "Fag bashers. Those fucking

heterosexual straight teenagers who need to take out their macho instincts as a large herd against lonely gay men. Fucking little bastards." I got the actual story with only a few more tirades thrown in. It wasn't much different from any other fag-bashing story. Four or five kids—he still wasn't sure how many—had attacked him outside a gay bar. He'd blown his police whistle, tried to run, fought like mad, all to no avail. "I managed to land a few punches." He licked his lips. "I nearly twisted the dick and balls off one of the little motherfuckers. I think that's when they broke my leg. I gave descriptions to the cops, but I'm sure they'll never catch the little no-neck monsters. They never do." He sighed dramatically. Ever the martyr, he'd milk this for as much sympathy as he could get.

Scott and I seldom get hassled by fag bashers. I suspect it's because we're big enough to give pause to all but the stupidest attackers. We talked for a while, found that his pride was hurt more than his physical self.

Before retracing our steps to my place, we cruised up Michigan Avenue. With the newly fallen snow, the thousands of lights strung on the trees along the avenue took on a glow beyond their usual magnificence. We could have stayed at Scott's in the city, but I had work the next day, and I didn't have a car for the drive to the suburbs. He had an engagement at noon at the Palmer House to speak to a Boys' Club. While we'd been talking to Neil, the snow had started. They'd predicted around two inches.

As we drove past Orland Square Mall, I saw Scott staring fixedly into the rearview mirror. "We're being followed," he said.

I sat up and looked back. "You sure?"

"Those same headlights have been behind us since One Hundred Eleventh Street, maybe before. They slow down and speed up when I do."

"Maybe they're following your tracks to keep on the road. They don't look like they've been plowed."

While there wasn't much snow, the wind was up, and drifts formed quickly in racing swirls on the roadway.

Through the rear window, I watched a semi-truck barreling toward us from the distance. It rushed past our follower, came up fast, and rocketed past us, raising new swirls of whiteness. "Stupid son of a bitch is going to end up in a ditch," Scott said.

I watched the headlights behind us. They followed sedately. "This is ridiculous," I said. "We don't do car chases. A blazing rush down the highway in the middle of winter is not something I want to try." I looked back again. "I'd like to find out who it is, though. Let's pull into Gas City on One Hundred Ninety-first Street. They'll have to make a choice by then. They can't hide with all that light."

They made their decision before then, however. As we neared Interstate 80, the other car sped up. They pulled even with us as we crossed over the expressway. I saw dim figures in a dark car but nothing else. They swerved toward us. Scott only tapped the brakes; still we hit an icy patch. Our car swung toward the bridge railing. Scott twisted the wheel. I grabbed on to the dashboard. The other car was now ahead of us. Its own acceleration and swerve toward us caused its driver to fight for control. I watched it swing over both lanes. Scott had the Porsche righted, continuing to tap the brakes. For a few seconds, we did a three-hundred-horsepower ballet. The brakes responded for a moment, then we began another skid. We traveled sideways for fifty feet toward the other car. I watched as its driver righted his car and sped off. Scott pulled the Porsche under control three feet from the brink of hurtling over the bridge onto the highway below.

We sat in silence a moment. "Thank Christ the idiot in the semi isn't around," Scott said. He U-turned at 191st Street and drove back toward my place. When I looked, no one followed us. I hadn't recognized anyone in the other car, nor was I able to make out the license-plate number.

I leaned my head back against the top of the seat. I let the furry cushion comfort me. "Let's go home," I said. "I need a long workout and a hot shower."

Working out is one of the sexiest turn-ons for both of us. I still fit into the gym shorts I wore when I played sports in high school. Scott's in great shape by profession.

When we started, the irons felt cold to the touch. In ten minutes, the chill wore off. In twenty minutes, the sweat flowed pleasingly. In half an hour, Scott's sweat pants clung to his crotch in warm, sensuous folds. The basement was too cool to linger in, however. After showers, we reclined on the couch in the living room in T-shirts, jockey shorts, and white gym socks. He's one of the few men I've seen whose briefs fit snugly around his ass.

I turned one lamp on low, inserted a Judy Collins CD, and lay down with my head in his lap. He smelled damp and clean and sexy. I caressed the hairs on the arm he draped over my chest. I left the curtains on the picture window open so we could watch the storm howl to its heart's content. Judy sang sweet and soft. I still go to her concerts every time she comes to Chicago.

Scott said, "I was afraid we'd lose it for a minute there."

"I had absolute faith in you and the car."

"I'm also glad we've got the security system here. I'd be even more glad if we were staying at my place."

"I guess we should have. I didn't think there'd be danger. Besides, we don't know if it's connected to the murder. It could have been some idiot teenager getting a few kicks.

"I hope that's all it was," he said.

He ran his fingers under the waistband of my shorts. I rubbed my face against the blond down on his stomach.

5

Scott promised to call the public defender to see whether his status or prestige or name recognition might get them to act more quickly in getting bail for Jeff.

The bitter cold ripped through my clothes as I ran from my car to the school. Another day when the high temperature might not get above zero.

Carolyn Blackburn met me at the school door.

"We've got a problem," she said. She walked me to my classroom. The door lay splintered in the hallway. A blizzard of chaos covered every inch of the room.

"The janitors discovered the break-in first thing this morning. They called the police and me. Someone vandalized your room and my office. The custodians started cleaning my office when the police left a half hour ago. They'll start in here next."

I had the same feeling of loss and vulnerability you get when your home is broken into. Carolyn stood in the doorway as I toured the wreckage. On the blackboard, someone had written, "What happened to Susan Warren can happen to you."

I touched the slashed and torn bulletin boards. I straightened the one desk still whole and standing. The spines had been ripped off all the books on the shelves. The famous-authors posters for which I'd paid ten dollars a piece lay in tattered ruins. Every drawer of every file cabinet lay exposed and empty, the contents tossed tornadically around the room.

Only a fool isn't frightened at the right moment, but I'd be goddamned if I'd be scared off. At first, it was helping Jeff and Mrs. Trask, one a student, the other a friend, but now it was personal; somebody was after me. That shit I would never put up with. Two janitors carried out the largest remnant of my desk. Carolyn and I were alone in the room.

She said, "I'm going to tell you this, but if you repeat it or say it came from me, I'll deny it and call you a liar."

I gave her a brief smile and nod that I understood.

She walked to the window and looked out. She began speaking with her back to me. "I've taught for years. I know how school systems work, how parents and boards put pressure on us. I don't think I'm naïve."

She turned around. "But in my twenty years as an administrator, I've never had an experience like I've had here with the Twitchells." She shook her head. "Dad is not rational when it comes to his daughter. From him, I get angry ravings. From the mother, I get that if I don't let up on her kid, I'll be in trouble."

She sat in the one desk, looked up at me, and pounded her hand softly on the fake wood surface. "That girl needs help. As much as I've ever seen in all these years."

She explained that when she'd come to Grover Cleveland, she'd watched carefully for potential problems. Early on, she'd discovered Becky was one of them. She talked to people. Those who would talk told her incredible stories. In seventh grade, in front of a whole class, Becky'd ripped all her textbooks to shreds after receiving an F for one quiz. The girl expressed no regret or remorse for this. The next day, her parents sent her with the money for an entire new set of books. Becky's cruelties at lunchtime were legendary—picking on the most unpopular boys or girls, humiliating them, reducing them to tears.

Earlier this year, a teacher tried to lead her by the elbow out of his classroom. It was after school and he had tried to counsel her on her irrational behavior. He claims it was a harmless, caring gesture. At the instant of contact, she screamed rape and began sobbing.

Carolyn shook her head. "Luckily, I'd been patrolling a nearby hall, and I got there before a crowd could gather. I'll never forget that first talk with her. A thirty-year-old hooker might talk like she did. Still, I detected a kid's vulnerability not far below the surface. I managed to defuse the situation for the unfortunate teacher. Becky is poison."

Carolyn had tried to check up on rumors and accusations that had followed Becky for years. "The few who dared confront her with this behavior," Carolyn said, "report that she seemed totally unconcerned about punishment or repercussions. Remorse seems to be the farthest thing from her mind. If a teacher did confront her, something would happen to them within twenty-four hours: car windows broken, materials stolen from their classrooms. Up to about eighth grade, the threat of telling her father usually had an effect." She shut her eyes and rubbed a hand across her chin, then shot me a look. "My guess would be some kind of abuse from the father, physical or mental, something. But she comes back with Mom's protection. She's got the game of playing one parent off against the other perfected beyond any art—she's the Picasso of manipulative kids. Something is very odd and very wrong there." She drummed her fingers on the desktop. "I'm stumped about what to do." She eyed me carefully, judging me on how much I could be trusted, I guessed. "Then, at ten o'clock last night, I got a call from the superintendent telling me to lay off Becky Twitchell. The warning from the superintendent was clear and genuine: Leave Becky alone. And I can't possibly prove abuse. No one anywhere has reported bruises, markings. Certainly, I've never seen such a thing."

In Illinois, teachers are required to report any case of suspected child abuse. Numerous times, I'd reported my suspicions, to see nothing come of them. The system here clanks along with as many inadequacies as anywhere else.

Carolyn said, "I've got a friend in the Department of Children and Family Services who I'll talk to about this, but I don't hold out much hope." She stood up. "And it's my first year on this job. I'd like to keep it to retirement. I don't know how far I'm willing to go with this." She gave me a wintry smile. "I've read your record, evaluations. You care about kids a great deal. In my limited way, I'll help you, but don't expect much. I know you don't trust me yet; no administrator could expect that."

We discussed possible ramifications of my involvement. She neither encouraged nor discouraged my talking to people, saying it was my decision. She explained that her goal was to help the kid if at all possible.

At least she'd been honest, a rare and valued commodity, something you didn't see in administrators very often. I told her I appreciated it.

Before she left, I got her to agree to take Roger Daniels and Doris Bradford out of their classes so I could talk to them during my first-period planning time. I met them in a blank-walled, gray-painted, cheerless room near the main office. The furniture consisted of a dull metal desk, matching dull metal chairs, and a black couch covered in cheap vinyl.

Doris came in first. She had long black hair to her waist—a slender cheerleader who'd been elected junior prom queen the year before. She wore tight blue jeans and a letterman's sweater. I'd never had her in class. I explained to her about helping Jeff.

Doris wouldn't give me even the benefit of nods and shakes of the head. I got monosyllabic mutterings and no information. After I finished with her, I might have been able to swear she'd been at Sunday's party, but not with any certainty. After ten minutes of fruitless questioning, I asked her who she thought might have a reason to kill Susan. She finally came to life, looked at me for the first and only time during the conversation.

"I don't have to answer your questions. You're not a lawyer. This isn't a court. You can't make me answer."

I took a stab in the dark. "Is that what Becky told you?"

After that, she clamped her mouth firmly shut, and I didn't get even monosyllables.

Roger shuffled in next. Almost as wide as he was tall, he moved awkwardly. He played starting left tackle on offense and defense on the football team. His brush-cut red hair glistened. I'd taught him freshman English. Back then, Roger'd been a shorter, squatter version of his present self. I told him what I was trying to do.

He squirmed in his seat, gazed at the barren gray walls, and looked over my shoulder to the parking lot outside. Finally, his eyes rested on me. He giggled. I'd never seen a six-foot block of teenage muscle omit such an incongruous sound. I asked him what he remembered about Sunday.

He hesitated, cleared his throat, gave me a pleading look. I said, "Roger, what the hell is going on?"

Finally, he said, "Mr. Mason, you've got to see what's happening. It's over the whole school about what happened to your classroom. If they can do that here in school, think what they could do to us."

"Who's they?"

"I can't tell you."

"Come on, Roger. You know I can be trusted."

"I know. But all the same, I can't tell you anything."

"Is Becky behind all this?"

He looked pained and defensive and didn't answer, but I presumed I was right.

"Who had a reason to kill Susan?"

"Nobody. She just hung around with us. I think the girls thought she was kind of okay. She was part of the crowd only because she dated Jeff."

I asked him about the possibility of drug or alcohol abuse at the party. I got nowhere with him on that topic. The bell rang for second hour. I could learn nothing more from him at that moment, so I let him go.

At noon, I called to see whether there'd been any progress in getting Jeff released. Mrs. Trask reported she'd be in court that afternoon. They'd managed to find a judge who would set a reasonable bail.

I expected Eric at four. In my restored room I spent the time after my tutoring group left wading through a stack of senior essays on Wordsworth and Coleridge. Seventeen- and eighteen-year-olds have amazingly weird notions about English Romantic poetry. I was halfway through the stack when Eric walked in. He arrived precisely on time.

Exceptionally lean and gawky, Eric was tall enough to be a basketball star, but uncoordinated enough to be stuck on the bench most of the time, when he wasn't ineligible because of his grades. Since graduation last June, he'd grown a mustache. His hair, more than fashionably long in back, was often gathered into a mini ponytail. On occasion, I'd seen him sporting a diamond stud earring. His thick eyebrows formed a straight line across his face, on which an ocean of zits mixed with scraggly wisps of beard.

He dumped his winter hat, coat, and gloves on a chair, along with his gym bag. He draped himself into a front-row seat. He wore designer jeans and a tight silk shirt. He'd obviously changed from his mechanic's work clothes. He moved his ass to the edge of the seat, planted his feet wide apart, and crossed his arms over his bony chest. He'd driven my car over. I offered him a ride home, but he said he'd stop at basketball practice and get a ride with one of the guys.

That out of the way, he said, "Jeff didn't kill her."

I could understand a brother standing up for his own, but he sounded absolutely definite.

"Who did?"

"Beats the hell out of me. Jeff may be a good athlete, tough and all, but he's got the soul of a nerd and the heart of a wimp.

Every time we wanted to do stuff, he'd wimp out. Like if me, Paul, and Roger wanted to go cruising to pick up girls, Jeff wouldn't go along. Said Susan was his girl and that was it. We were doing it just for fun. Nobody ever got lucky. But you never know, you might." His grin revealed uneven teeth. "I'd say he was pretty much by himself. He hung around with us, but he said the least."

"What about his temper?"

"We had fights. All brothers do." He shrugged. "He loses it pretty quick at games, that's all."

"That doesn't sound wimpy to me."

"Yeah, it is. He loses his temper over crybaby stuff. He only makes the refs mad. He sees the college and NBA guys do it on TV, and he thinks it's okay. It's bush-league bullshit."

"How was he Sunday? His usual self?"

"All he did was try to get Susan to leave early. We all ragged at him about it. He got kind of mad. He and Paul almost got into it. Nothing came of it. They sort of wrestled for a minute, but they ended up laughing."

Eric talked for a few minutes about Jeff's performance on the basketball court. Jeff was an above-average player except when his father showed up. His dad tended to yell and carry on, causing his son to freeze on the court. Soon after Dad would start, Jeff lost his temper over something in the game. Eric said, "I don't see the big deal about being yelled at. Montini does it all game every game. On the bench, we used to laugh behind his back. On the court, the starters ignore him. I guess Jeff can tune out the coach, but it's hard to ignore my dad, he's such a pig."

Eric laughed. "Montini used to yell at me because I'm six eight, and I think he had visions of state championships with me as a center. But I'm a klutz and stupid. It took him a couple years to get used to that."

"Your mom said Coach Windham called."

He looked surprised and guilty. "That was to see if he could help Jeff." All my teacher instincts told me he lied. I wished I knew why.

I asked how Montini treated the kids, especially Jeff and Paul. Eric said that the ones colleges recruited got special attention and extra practices. Also, Paul, Jeff, and some of these guys hung around after practice to bullshit with Montini. The coach wanted to get kids placed in colleges. Montini told them his dream was to coach at a major university, then the pros. It seemed that the more players he placed in colleges, the better his chances were of moving up.

The last few losing seasons must have driven him nuts. More loses, less recruiting, I guessed.

Eric concluded, "I like the guys on the team. That's why I was there Sunday. I've known Paul since grade school. I'm two years older than he is, but he was always on our teams because he was so good."

I asked about Susan.

"She's quiet. Never bothered me. Seemed to be more with it this year." He shrugged. "I can't figure why somebody'd want to kill her."

"I've been having trouble with the other kids. They won't talk about what happened Sunday."

"They're worried about Becky. She talked to everybody, me included. She wants us to keep our mouths shut."

"Why?"

"It's hard to tell with Becky. She's pretty weird. She threatened to get revenge on anybody who cooperated with you. She lives in a dopey little world of cops and robbers, good guys and bad guys."

"How'd she threaten you?"

"She said she'd tell about the time I 'borrowed' a car last month."

"You're not back to stealing cars!" I said.

When he was a freshman, one of the cars he'd stolen had been mine. I told you he wasn't too bright. Even back then, my car had a penchant for breaking down at inopportune moments. When it was stolen, it chose to die a block from school. He'd been seen by half the student body either when he'd taken the car, while driving it, or as he kicked at it when it wouldn't go. Rust now covered most of the places he'd managed to dent in his frustration. I didn't turn him in to the cops. I wound up talking to him about it. When he got arrested for the same thing several years later, the cops wouldn't turn him over to his buddies who tried to bail him out. He refused to call his parents, so he'd tried me. I'd shown up, saved his ass. I've already mentioned the drug incident, which occurred a few months later. He'd promised to get help.

Now he shook his head vigorously. "Honest, Mr. Mason, I really borrowed it from a guy. He's a good friend. You don't know him. He told me I could use it anytime. I took his word. As soon as he found out it was me, everything was cool."

If Becky called the police about it, I didn't think they could do anything to Eric, but she could cause him some trouble. If he got arrested again, he was due for a trip to Stateville.

He scratched his head. "Becky is one tough nut. I think she's dangerous."

I waited for him to continue. He tugged on the earring in his left ear, sat up straighter. "I've always trusted you, from the first time when you didn't turn me in for taking your car." I nodded. "You can't say anything about what I tell you or where you heard it."

I promised.

"Becky's the school's biggest drug pusher. She's afraid with all the cops around, she'll lose business, maybe even get caught. That's why she called everybody. She runs the whole drug operation. I think she's afraid the cops'll uncover the whole thing if they investigate the murder." He tugged on a wisp of beard. "Rumor has it she sells to teachers."

That kids made drug deals in school did not surprise me. I

knew faculty members did drugs, George Windham being an obvious example. "Are you sure she's the main pusher?" I asked.

"Everybody says it. I've seen her deal a lot at our parties, and a couple times in the school parking lot when I came to pick up some buddies."

"Which teachers does she sell to?"

He twisted his fingers together, cracked his knuckles in one jerky motion.

"You've gone this far," I prompted.

"Yeah, I guess." He rattled off a list of seven or eight faculty members, among them Pete Montini and George Windham. Most were younger teachers, new to the district, whom I didn't know.

"Were Jeff or Susan involved in the drug pushing?"

"Not that I ever knew."

"Do you know anything about how Becky's system worked or where she got it from?"

This time, he got up and strolled to the window. He cracked his knuckles several more times as he stared at the snow outside. Finally, he turned back. "I hate that bitch so much. You really can't say anything to anybody."

I renewed my promise of discretion.

"I mean she can take real revenge. I know one guy who crossed her. He wound up with his dad's new Mercedes in Lake Michigan. Somebody ran him off Lake Shore Drive. The kids say it was Becky, but nobody could prove anything. He was lucky to get out alive."

He sighed and sat back down. He started to crack his knuckles again.

"Don't, please," I said.

He grinned at me. "Sorry. Anyway, supposedly there's this farmhouse about an hour or so west of here. It's like a supply depot or something. Everybody's heard about it, but nobody's actually been except Becky."

It really wasn't a lot of help, not terribly specific, and I didn't see how it hooked in with Susan's death—unless her murder was connected with some kind of drug war, which made little sense, and for which I had no proof. I'd have to keep asking around. Eric knew no more. After extracting repeated promises to say nothing to anyone, he left.

Scott had an afternoon engagement at a hospital, visiting AIDS patients and giving out toys to kids, so he wouldn't be picking me up until six. I didn't want to leave in my car and miss him. I graded papers for a while, finally finishing last week's stacks. I began working on my packet of negotiations materials. We had a meeting scheduled during Christmas vacation.

I'd gotten five pages into it when I felt another presence in the room. It was Carolyn Blackburn. Scott stood behind her.

"I got done early," he said. "I wasn't sure where your room was."

"I needed to speak to you, so I came down with him," Carolyn said.

Carolyn stood in front of my desk. Her gray eyes looked grim; her mouth was set in a firm line. "I got another call from the superintendent," she said. "I quote: 'Inform Mr. Mason he is not to harass any of the students or faculty about the Susan Warren murder. A school board member has complained.' "

Superintendent Oliver Sandgrace, in office less than a year, I'd never met. I'd seen him at a distance. All I'd noticed was that when he smiled, he had gaps between upper and lower front teeth. I'd heard he was a former physical-education teacher from farm country near Galena, Illinois, on the Mississippi River.

Scott perched on the window ledge. Carolyn pulled a student's desk closer to mine and sat down.

I raised an eyebrow. "I'd be happy to meet with whoever's complaining and talk it over."

"Boards don't work like that, Tom. You should know that after all these years."

"How do they work?" Scott asked.

She smiled wearily. "People generally get elected to a school board because some faction in the community is mad about one issue. Once on the board, they discover that it's a lot of meetings about intricate and boring financial responsibilities. Their one issue fades, and they find themselves in the morass of educational silliness involving state mandates, useless reforms, contradictory regulations, and that doesn't even talk about the federal government's convolutions."

"Why do they stay?" Scott asked.

"They love to meddle," I said. I explained that most board members learn to sit at meetings and vote for what the superintendent recommends. They aren't financial planners or budgetary experts. They're housewives, mechanics, good people mostly, but they have to rely on those they hire. That's a simplification, but it sums up the basics. What's left is their status in the community. Drunk on minuscule power and minimal expertise, they spend time listening to the complaints of their neighbors. They want to be liked and popular and get reelected, so they tell their neighbors they can take care of the problems, like some ward boss in Chicago. It's a power trip.

In some districts, board members call and administrators jump. In many schools, the philosophy is give the board members whatever they want, no matter whether the decision is educationally sound or not.

I've known board members who've used their position simply to keep their quite average students in honors classes; and they blame the teachers of those same groups when their C + children inevitably fail. Of course, some teachers have caught on to this game, too. A few toady up to board members, give their kids A's, and tell the parents what they want to hear. We've got one elderly teacher, in the district since day one, who's made a career out of giving easy grades. The parents love her. As Mark Twain said, "In the first place God made idiots. This was for practice. Then He made school boards."

I concluded, saying, "Some administrators let parents walk all over the teachers and themselves."

"Tom's being overly dramatic and a little harsh, but not all that inaccurate. They like to meddle, to show off their power, and to be anonymous and mysterious."

"They prefer to frighten the accused into compliance," I said, "rather than openly confront those who may have displeased them."

"That's bullshit," Scott said.

"That's life in the educational system," I said. "Witness the current situation with Mrs. Twitchell as president of the school board."

"Yes, that's the immediate problem," Carolyn said. "I presume Mrs. Twitchell called. The superintendent talked to me. He asked me to meet with you. You're supposed to stop."

"The board voted?" I asked.

"Can they do that?" Scott asked.

Carolyn drummed her fingers on the desktop. "They couldn't have voted. They don't meet until next month. Can they do it? I don't know. The message is to stop."

"Do you want me to stop?"

"It's not my decision."

"Should I meet with Sandgrace? Try to work it out with him?"

"You can try. I doubt if it would do any good."

"It's a cover-up," Scott declared. "It's got to be Twitchell and her goddamn daughter."

Carolyn cleared her throat. "I'd say that's a shrewd guess. But the superintendent didn't tell me. I won't hinder you. I can't promise any help, and I can't guarantee that you won't be in deep trouble if you continue."

On the way out, we stopped in the teachers' lounge. I called Frank Murphy to see how bail had gone. The lawyers had done a great job. Jeff had been released to his mom around four.

As I put on my coat, I told Scott what I'd learned that day.

"Practice should be just about over," I concluded. "I want to confront Windham and Montini here tonight."

The empty corridors echoed our footsteps as we strode to the gym. It was empty. No lights shone. We made our way to the locker room. We heard random bangings. A few kids remained, combing their hair or bundling into winter coats. In Montini's office, Paul Conlan and a couple others remained talking to the coaches. I presumed these were the ones Eric referred to as the ones who hung around Montini. Scott's presence caused a minor stir among the kids. He signed a few autographs. I thought our presence seemed to disturb Montini greatly. George sat coolly, thumping a basketball while he rested his ass on the top of a desk. Montini rushed the kids out and told us he was in a hurry.

Dimly lit and oppressively humid, the locker room gloomed around us. This section of Grover Cleveland had been built during the Depression. Rows of gray metal lockers muted the distant sound of dripping, ancient showers. The smell of rotting jockstraps oozed into your nostrils. Trophies, charts, and old, dirty brown basketballs cluttered most of the flat surfaces in Montini's tiny cubicle of an office.

Montini wore a T-shirt cut off at the midriff, with an ubiquitous cartoon cat on the front. The shirt revealed a quarter-sized mole with hair growing out of it an inch above his navel. He said, "I really have to leave, you guys." He whiped off the T-shirt. The hair on the mole was the only hair he had on his chest. He threw on a sweat shirt and grabbed his coat from the top of a filing cabinet.

Windham watched this performance with an amused smirk on his face. He wore a bright yellow warm-up suit.

"We need to talk," I said.

"There's nothing to talk about," George Windham said very softly.

"My wife expects me home," Pete Montini said.

"You guys can't hide what's wrong forever," I said.

"There's nothing wrong, and we're not hiding anything," George said smoothly. "I can't imagine what you're talking about."

"Drugs and kids," I said.

George laughed and said, "Don't be absurd.

Pete's face turned beet red. "You motherfuckers," he said.

George stopped him. "We have nothing to say." He reached for his coat, leaned past my head, and flicked off a row of light switches. Now only the emergency lights gave a soft glow. The natural dimness became eerie and tinged with danger. George began ushering Pete out the door.

"You two can stay as long as you like," George said. "Just be sure to close the door when you leave."

"You told me yesterday, George—" I began

He turned on me, for once his voice raised. "I told you what? Do you have a witness, a tape, some kind of proof? I'm not responsible for what you make up."

"What are you guys afraid of?"

"Nothing," George said breezily. They were two-thirds of the way out of the locker room before I could think of anything to say, and by then it was too late.

Outside the wind howled at a gale. Icy flurries roared by in horizontal bursts. It had to be well below zero. The wind slammed the snow into swirling drifts. We hurried to the car. The interior was frigid, the seat shockingly cold on my ass. Scott started the car and got the heater going. He said, "Supposed to hit record cold tonight, with another storm. I thought it wasn't supposed to snow when it was this cold."

"Somebody lied to you," I said. Growing up in southern Alabama had not prepared him for Chicago at fifteen below.

"That little scene in there was a fiasco," I said.

"They're scared shitless, especially Pete," Scott said. "I can't believe a teacher buying drugs from kids. That is major-league stupid. You going to report it?"

"I doubt it. I've got no real proof." Scott's Porsche had quickly reached a comfortable warmth. "Let's go eat first and come back for my car later. Then I want to try to talk to some parents tonight. I haven't had the greatest luck with the kids; maybe I can learn something from the parents."

Scott swung the car out of the parking lot. I gazed at the cold brick mass of the darkened school as we moved down the drive to 167th Street. A shadow darker than the others caught my eye. It was out of place. I stared hard.

"Stop the car," I said.

He braked. "What?"

I peered out. Snow swirled for a minute, blocking my view of the school. The wind died for a few moments. "I've been teaching here sixteen years and that shadow's never been there before." I pointed.

"I don't see anything," Scott said. "It's probably just a snow-drift."

I already had the car door open, however. "Wait. I'm going to check it out." I hurried the thirty-five feet to the wall. I heard Scott's car door slam, listened to the crunch of his feet through the snow behind me.

Two feet from the school, in a valley between two rapidly growing drifts, was a body, face turned away from me, coat wide open, with no hat or gloves on. With a wind chill factor of seventy below zero, exposed skin could freeze in minutes.

6

I bent over the body and turned the head. It was Eric. I leaned closer, put my hand on his chest, felt it barely rise and fall.

Strong as we are and as good shape as we're in, it was still a struggle to carry Eric into the school. I called the paramedics and Mrs. Trask. We followed the ambulance to Palos Community Hospital. We met Mrs. Trask in the emergency room.

We grabbed a bite to eat in the hospital cafeteria, and went back to check on Eric. The doctor said the boy was in poor shape. He'd only been in the cold a few minutes, she thought, but the danger of frostbite was great. He might lose several fingers at least. They wouldn't know for a few days. He'd also been badly beaten and had three broken ribs. He was under sedation. We could see him the next day. We talked to the police, listened to Mrs. Trask's complaints, and left.

We went back to get my car. It was only seven but the streets were nearly deserted. Scott's car glided easily over icy patches and through rapidly building drifts. When we'd found Eric, there hadn't been time for more than a perfunctory glance around.

Back at school, we found any search was useless. I wanted to find Eric's gym bag. In the time since we'd found him, the snow had completely drifted over all traces of what had happened. We hunted in a wide arc out from the school but couldn't find his bag.

Scott followed as I drove my car to my place. Back in his car, I said, "Was this Becky's revenge?"

"How could she know he told and what he told? Could she be that efficient? Found out so quick and had an attack carried out?"

I shrugged. "We'll know more after we talk to Eric tomorrow. For now, I want to see the Conlans and Twitchells." While going through the files, I'd written down the home addresses and phone numbers of all the kids and adults involved. Mr. Conlan sat on the River's Edge school board. We drove to the Conlans'.

Paul answered the door. With a confused look, he let us in. The Conlans lived in the exclusive area of River's Edge, newly built and filled with newly rich. Every home cost over four hundred thousand dollars. I explained that we wanted to talk to his parents.

He shuffled nervously for a few moments, but his parents solved the problem of their availability by entering the room. I made introductions and explained that we wanted to talk to them. Mrs. Conlan looked refined, elegant, and brittle. Her hair, makeup, and outfit were as clean, set, and pressed as if she were ready for luncheon rather than for an evening at home. Mr. Conlan wore baggy old pants, a dumpy sweater, and a genial smile. His slippers flopped on the tile as he led us to a sitting room. Paul tried to follow, but his dad waved him away. He told him the adults needed to talk.

Mrs. Conlan sat primly on the edge of a grimly brown settee. Mr. Conlan stood to her left and a little behind. All the furniture cluttered around may have been genuine antiques. As far as I knew, it could have been complete junk. Either way, I guessed we were supposed to be aware of how expensive it was. None of it seemed to match. The LeRoy Neiman sport scene hanging on the wall behind them contributed to the feeling that we were in a *Better Homes and Gardens* disaster area. Mrs. Conlan touched her blond hairdo, rearranging nothing. She said, "I don't see why you're here. We've talked to the police quite enough. Paul has been sufficiently upset as it is. Just because the poor girl and that hideous boy were here before it happened is no reason to continue harassing us. Can't the children get together for a little innocent fun on a Sunday afternoon without all kinds of people making a horrible issue of it?"

"I wouldn't call murder innocent fun," I said.

The wispy wave of her hand dismissed my comment. Mr. Conlan stopped any retort of hers. He said, "Dear, perhaps you didn't catch Mr. Carpenter's name."

She patted her hair again. "Is that important, Harold, when we're talking about our son?"

"Mr. Carpenter is a professional baseball player, dear. He's quite famous, a major sports star. I believe the papers have mentioned he owns a penthouse on Lake Shore Drive."

"Really." Her tone was more accommodating now. "Perhaps you could help Paul with his career. He's practiced very hard since he was nine. He studies, too, of course. He's not a dummy. My father and brothers were athletes." She gave a little cough, meant to be demure, I guessed. "I, of course, was a cheerleader." She gave a little titter, then continued. "We want him to follow in the family tradition. Of course, he'll go to the best college and get an education. He'll need something to fall back on when his professional career is behind him."

"Perhaps Mr. Carpenter would endorse the opera benefit," her husband said.

"I'd be delighted," Scott said.

"You would?" The titter returned, this time behind one of her hands. "I'll just step into the study and get the information." She bustled out the door.

Mr. Conlan's face split into a slow, easy grin. He was gray-haired and I guessed in his mid-fifties. "She'll be gone a few minutes, so we can get something accomplished. She means well. She gets Paul mixed up with her father, her brothers, and her ego. Don't get me wrong, I want Paul to succeed, but at what *he* wants. I think this pressure is wrong."

"Mr. Conlan," I began.

"Call me Harry."

"Harry," I corrected. "We wanted to find out more about Sunday." I explained about Jeff and helping with the investigation.

"I can't tell you much. We had the monthly meeting with the Sports Boosters, then we attended one of Sylvia's charity benefits. We got home quite late. News of the murder had already reached here before then."

"Did anybody chaperon the Sunday parties?"

"My wife and I would stop in occasionally. The kids came here, you know, because we have the largest TV screen. This last year, they added girls to the company. I guess sports can keep boys from discovering girls only just so long."

"Did they do drugs or alcohol at the parties?"

"I never saw any. I trust Paul implicitly. He's never betrayed my trust in him. Being kids in today's world, I suspect they did some experimenting."

"I know it's none of my business, but I'm curious about Paul's relationship with Becky Twitchell."

He frowned. "The girl is a problem. She always seems to have her hands all over him."

Mrs. Conlan rolled in a portable bar. She'd heard her husband's last comment. "You must be talking about that hideous Becky Twitchell," she said. "After every visit from her, something is missing from this house. I know it's her who's stealing. I've warned Paul about her numerous times. She's nothing but trouble."

"You called Jeff hideous earlier," I said to her.

"Isn't a murderer hideous?" she asked.

"He hasn't had a trial yet," I said. I got a nasty look for that crack. I hurried to ask, "Did you know Susan Warren?"

"She was not the right sort at all. I commented many times to my husband, never in front of the poor girl, of course, that she dressed in rags. She wasn't even up to K-Mart. She was hardly our concern, but that Becky girl was."

"Becky used to mouth off to my wife a great deal. I stayed out of the child's way. I told my wife any nasty comments she made would simply drive Paul and Becky together."

"My husband understands young people so much better than I." Her brittle smile hid any disagreement.

We left a few moments later, refusing refreshment even though Mrs. Conlan pressed us. She beamed when we left, though. Scott'd agreed to attend an opera benefit in January.

"The things I do for you," he said in the car. "I'm going to the opera. I hate opera. There're going to be fat ladies with low-cut dresses bellowing to the last balcony."

"And opera queens who will swoon over you."

"Shit."

"Maybe you'll learn to like opera."

"Maybe I'll flap my arms and fly to the moon."

The snow had worsened, but the wind had let up a little. It was eight-thirty, early enough to stop in at the Twitchells'.

As we drove, Scott said, "I liked Mr. Conlan. He didn't seem rushed or driven, more laid-back, cool."

I reminded him that Mrs. Trask had said nasty things about Paul's parents.

"Speaking of nasty, aren't you afraid the Twitchells will cause problems at work? Mrs. Twitchell does seem to be behind the pressure there."

"When have you known me to put up with bullshit from work?"

"Not often."

"And it's not starting tonight. My guess is lots of these people have something to hide. I want to find out what it is and if it's connected to the murder."

On the car radio, the announcer on WBBM, an all-news station, claimed it would stop snowing soon. They predicted twenty below by morning. Out the car window, it looked as if it would snow until the end of the next ice age. Scott's car purred through the storm. We were almost the only ones on the road.

An angry Mr. Twitchell let us in. We explained why we'd come.

He said. "Where's Becky? That tramp is out there somewhere in this chaos. She's never home. She's pulled this for the last time." They lived in the older section of River's Edge, north of the Forest Preserve. Dark wood paneling crept halfway up the walls. We talked in the foyer, coats on. He hadn't invited us in farther.

"You're overreacting, Fred. She'll call." A woman's voice preceded a tall striking-looking woman. She introduced herself to us. Mrs. Twitchell was a stark contrast to her short, freckled husband. She had to be in her forties, but she tried for an early-twenties look. She wore the worst-fitting clothes I'd ever seen, her pants clinging tighter than a taut rubber band. If she had any taste, she'd have made it to the level of cheap whore. As it was, one needed an eye shield, or preferably a blindfold, to protect one's sensibilities from the clashing apple green and hot pink color scheme and mismatched styles.

She pointed an elegantly painted maroon fingernail at me. "What are you doing here?" She could have been her own snowstorm of cold. "Weren't you told to leave Becky alone?"

"Don't cover for her again, Sally," he said.

"You'll loose your temper again," she said. "You know what the doctor says about overexerting yourself."

"He didn't know I had a slut for a daughter."

She turned to us. "It's time for you gentlemen to leave."

"We wanted to talk about Becky," I said.

"She needs a strong hand, tough discipline to keep her in line. Sally's coddled her for years. That's the problem."

Mrs. Twitchell added another twenty chilly degrees to her tone as she responded to him. "You can't see that she's a young woman who needs to become independent."

"Independent, horseshit. She runs you. She'd like to run this house. Who pays the bills around here?"

I tried a question. "Where's Becky tonight?"

"Whoring with that Conlan boy," Mr. Twitchell said.

"We just saw him at his house not more than a half hour ago," I said.

"She was hiding there," he said. "He's lied for her before. He's got one thing on his mind."

"You think that because it's all you have on your mind," Mrs. Twitchell said.

I tried a different question. "Do you know anything about Becky's whereabouts Sunday?"

"I think that's enough questions," Mrs. Twitchell said. "Our daughter, as should be abundantly clear to you, is none of your concern."

This touched off another domestic barrage that looked ready to escalate into total war. We beat a hasty retreat.

Scott let me drive. I love the feel of the Porsche under my control. I suppose it's juvenile. I'm the only one who's had it up over one hundred miles an hour.

"That was a disaster," Scott said.

As we neared 167th Street on LaGrange Road, I noticed a car in the rearview mirror. I changed lanes, slowed down, put my turn signals on. The car followed relentlessly. I tapped Scott and pointed. "I think we're being followed," I said.

"Again." Scott sounded bored.

I drove past our turnoff on 179th Street. The other car made no move over the I–80 bridge as before. We passed a lumbering oil tanker just before the road narrowed to two lanes past 191st Street. The other car screeched around the tanker. In my rearview mirror, I watched the truck jackknife and skid to a stop ten feet from the window of Fleckstein's Bakery. We caught the light on orange at Willow Lane. The other car sped through on red. I gazed carefully at it in the rearview mirror. It didn't look like the car from the night before.

"It's time to end this shit," I said.

"What are you going to do?"

"I think it's time to push this car a little. I recommend hanging on tight."

At St. Francis Road, without slowing or signaling, I wrenched the car into a sharp left. Oncoming traffic screeched angrily. Our shadow followed us. St. Francis Road curves and winds. It has two exceptionally dangerous spots for speeding cars. The first is in front of the Convent of the Franciscan Sisters of the Sacred Heart. I made the Porsche take this at sixty-five. The tires held, but the curve is blind and the oncoming car missed us by a foot at most. His horn blared until he realized there was someone right behind us. He settled slowly into the snowbank on the south side of the road. Our follower righted his swerving car and came on fast.

"I didn't think we did car chases," Scott said.

"What the hell. Why not?" I replied.

"What if he starts shooting?" Scott asked.

"Then I suspect this little car will go even faster."

We gained on him as we flew toward the S curve just before Eightieth Avenue. The curve exists because of a farmhouse that sits on a twenty-foot bluff.

"Motherfucker," Scott muttered. I glanced at him. His eyes were closed, his hands gripped the dashboard, braced for a crash. I glanced in the rearview mirror. We were still gaining. We hit the first leg of the curve, tires screaming. We jolted against the snowdrift on the left. The Porsche swung 360 degrees, paused, swayed. I gunned the engine. The car leapt through the second leg of the S, picking up speed as we drew away.

"Could we not do that again for a while?" Scott said.

We passed a car filled with kids heading toward the curve. I pointed. "I'm more worried about them. Two cars can barely take that curve at normal speed. If our tracker is there, it's going to be bloody and we'll need to help the victims."

I swung onto Eightieth Avenue, pulled into the farmhouse driveway, and snapped off the lights. No light shone in the house.

I inched to the end of the driveway to look down at the S curve. The kid-filled car sat half in the ditch, its driver out and shouting. Our follower backed and maneuvered to ease past him. I rolled my window down to catch anything that was said.

I waited for the one car to maneuver past the other. In the headlight glare, it looked like a Trans Am.

Another car entered the curve and paused. This driver asked the guy blocking the road whether he needed any help. The first driver said everybody was okay, and he'd call for a tow from his car phone.

"Let's get out while we can," Scott said.

"Nonsense. We're going to follow him."

He frowned. "I'm not sure I have the nerve for that kind of thing."

"We're about to find out," I said.

It took precious seconds to turn around in the farmer's front yard. At the end of the driveway, I glanced around. No one going east on St. Francis Road. I was afraid we'd lost him. Then I saw red taillights top a rise going north on Eightieth Avenue. I jammed the car into gear and rushed off after our pursuer.

Scott said, "Let me check this to make sure I've got it absolutely clear. We are racing at"—he eyed the speedometer— "at ninety miles per hour after someone who may be trying to kill us. This is the coldest winter in a hundred years. With the wind chill, it's at least seventy below out. There are ice and snow patches everywhere on the roads, any one of which could hurtle us into oblivion."

"You worry too much; besides, you've got your seat belt on."

"That's a comfort. I want you to realize I'm just checking, not criticizing. However, if this gets us killed, I may raise one or two objections."

"We're closer," I whispered. I eased off the gas pedal. "It's one guy, I think." I settled down to follow him.

"Why are we whispering?" Scott whispered.

"I've never trailed someone who was trailing me. I've got goose bumps."

"Or rocks in your head."

"Maybe both." He turned left on 191st Street. "I don't want any dramatic confrontations. I want to see where he goes, maybe see who it is."

"He could spot us. He may have a gun."

"I'll stop if you want. Seriously." The other guy turned right, onto LaGrange Road.

Scott grumbled, "You're sticking this on my shoulders."

"This has to be by unanimous consent. It's deadly and dangerous. I vote yes."

He sighed. "You better watch the road. He's turning onto the Interstate."

The car ahead raced onto the ramp going west toward Joliet. We followed. He sped up to seventy-five and left it there to cruise. I dropped several cars behind, hiding behind a semi-truck or two. Enough cars broke the speed limit along with us to keep us hidden, I hoped. In one of winter's oddities, the road remained remarkably clear of snow. The wind howled straight out of the west. North-south roads might be difficult to drive, but for now, the highway was clear. Our pursuer didn't slow down through the 45-mph speed zone in Joliet. Then again, nobody else ever does, either. Through Joliet and past the interchange with I-55, we sped into the night. Here fewer cars offered us protection from discovery. I feared we were too far behind. We could easily miss him if he turned off; but on he went and on we followed. Fifty minutes past I-55, he pulled off at the Ottowa exit. He sped south. The country roads slowed him. Even though the road had recently been plowed, drifts rapidly shifted back over it. We played cat and mouse through the sparse traffic into Grand Ridge, and then drove five more miles, until he turned onto a private drive. I drove past, then doubled back. I paused a half mile beyond the entrance.

"Now what?" Scott asked.

"We go exploring."

"I don't remember skulking about in the dark as being part of the agreement when we became lovers."

"Shows what you know. It's right there after who has to take out the garbage on winter weekends."

"Is not."

I whumped his shoulder. It couldn't hurt through all that winter-coat padding. "I'll show you when we get back; until then, we've come this far. We might as well see the whole show. I promise if it looks even slightly dangerous, we'll go back, get in the car, and go home."

He sighed. A bright half-moon and a star-filled sky above the wind-driven snow gave enough light to show the indecision in his rugged jaw.

"Come on, big guy." He hesitated a little longer, then caught my eyes and held them. Finally, he nodded.

I drove the car as far off the shoulder as I dared, to keep it hidden. I had confidence in its front-wheel drive to get us out of any deep drifts. Gravel crunched under our feet as we walked the fifty yards to the opening of the driveway. No cars passed us. A cloudless sky loomed above, but at ground level, the wind whipped snow at a violent pace. Rivulets of drifts spread slowly across the road. Waves of white swept over our feet and disappeared down the road.

A thin sheet of ice covered the gravel driveway almost completely. Glassy ice from the last semithaw filled the potholes. From the road, we couldn't see the farther end of the driveway, but we could make out lights in the distance.

Barren black trees, branches whipping in the wind, lined each side of the driveway. Even with the clear moonlight and starlight, we stumbled over ruts and bumps.

"They could at least have paved the damn thing for us," Scott muttered. He was muffled from head to toe. I could barely see the slits where his eyes shone. At times, the wind blew the snow stinging into our eyes. By the time we got to the end of the driveway, my eyes had watered enough to form icicles on the scarf I had wrapped around my face. It took more than fifteen minutes, a sudden turn bringing us to within five feet of the back of the Trans Am that had been following us. Painted flat black, it radiated a sinister warmth. I could hear the faint clicking of the cooling engine. Having nothing to write with, I repeated the license number in my head five or six times.

We crouched behind the car and examined the vista in front of us. I lowered my scarf for a better view. Straight ahead, maybe twenty yards, stood a rambling old farmhouse, three stories tall, with numerous additions that had pushed the building far beyond its original shape. Lights shone in the house on the first floor only. I couldn't see anyone moving inside. To our right, maybe thirty yards beyond the house, a haphazardly renovated old barn wheezed and groaned in the wind. A circular drive led past the house and around the barn. An unshoveled path led directly from the car to the house. Only one set of footprints disturbed the drifts toward the front door.

To our left, the woods made a wide circle and then drew within ten feet of the house. We inched in that direction. Our feet crunched frighteningly loudly in the darkness, but the noise of the wind would cover our passage, I hoped.

We crept past the car. I glanced inside. The dark interior told me nothing.

We inched along among the trees. Stealth in the Vietnam jungles was never like this, but the training then served me now. The woods provided enough cover for me to feel safe. I heard Scott's low breathing behind me. He moved less than two feet away. The wind pulled away the sound of our feet crunching on the snow. Someone could have been following us at five feet and I wouldn't have heard them. However, my jungle training —something I'd never lost, all those instincts I didn't want to remember—came back. I was wary, alert, and I hoped a little dangerous. At the near point to the house, we stopped to reconnoiter. Two feet from the house, barren bushes made an ice-covered picket fence. A light shone through the first-floor window closest to the front. I put my lips next to where Scott's ear most likely was inside his blue knit cap. "I want to get a closer look," I said. "Stay here."

I left before he could object. I rushed across the expanse of coverless darkness and stopped an inch from the house, almost slipping on the ice that pooled close to the foundation bricks. I slid-tiptoed closer to the window. Slowly, I raised my head, every sense alert to any possible movement. At the moment, the wind presented the largest problem. It whipped around this side of the house in a gale. Again, my eyes stung with the wind-driven snow. I feared that the constant watering might prevent me from seeing.

I crouched over. With one hand, I gripped the windowsill. I placed my other hand against the house, felt it slip, caught myself. I planted my feet as carefully as possible. I raised my head millimeter by millimeter toward the windowsill. My left eye appeared over the rim of the sill a minute before the other. I saw a wall covered with bookcases directly opposite me. In front of it sat a massive desk, the large wooden type they made for schoolteachers before they discovered cheap plastic or steel ones.

I turned my head left an inch. I glimpsed a barren wall with a doorway in the middle leading to the darkened room beyond. I switched back to the right with painful slowness. Holding such a tight position began to strain my muscles. I'd have to leave in a few minutes. To the right, I saw Pete Montini standing on one side of a fireplace, head down, fists clenched. On the other side of the fireplace was a man I didn't recognize. He towered to at least six foot nine. He wore baggy painter pants, a red-checked flannel shirt opened at the throat to reveal a long-sleeved winter T-shirt, the ends of which shown at his wrists. He shook his extended hand, finger pointing, an inch from Pete's face. I couldn't hear their words.

Between them on a rug in front of the fireplace lay a German shepherd puppy. His head lay on his paws, his eyes flicking to the two humans above. I hoped his well-trained mother or father wasn't around.

Pete raised a hand as if pleading. The other slammed his fist on the mantelpiece. Pete flushed red. He shook his head no over and over. He seemed to be wilting under the bullying of the other. The stranger raised a hand to slap Pete. At that moment, my straining muscles began to give way. I caught myself with my left hand on the windowsill. An eternity later, I breathed. I looked again. Pete held the side of his face. The dog's head was up, ears at attention, eyes staring to the window where I perched. Time to leave: young or not, trained or not, I didn't want to wrestle with a German shepherd and his overly large master. I turned to steal away. My foot slipped. I caught myself for an instant, felt myself falling, grabbed a bush. It held, but my feet began to slide sideways. An instant later, my left leg gave a solid thump against the wall. Immediately, the dog roared to life. For a puppy, he sounded like a regiment. I dashed for the cover of the trees. Halfway across the glaring openness, floodlights bathed the entire perimeter of the house as bright as daylight. I heard doors slamming, loud shouting.

In the shelter of the trees, I searched frantically for Scott. I heard a shotgun blast, felt the pellets whiz past my head. I ducked down. "Scott!" I whispered. Stumbling and sliding, I hurried toward the Trans Am and the beginning of the driveway. I didn't want to chance a direct dash through the woods and possibly risk getting lost with a dog on my trail, followed by at least one man with a shotgun. Where was Scott? Then I heard a hoarse whisper behind me. I recognized Scott's muffled yelps. I stopped. Making no attempt to be quiet, he stumbled into the tree that I was hiding behind. The lights from the house let us see far enough into the woods to make our way along the perimeter. Scott said, "What the hell?" The shotgun boomed.

"Later. Run." Forgetting quiet or attempts at concealment,

we raced for the driveway, then rushed back the way we had come. The ice on the drive proved nastily treacherous because of our haste. Twice I slipped. Once Scott fell in a heap. I dragged him up and we kept going. I heard the car behind us roar to life.

"Through here," I shouted to Scott. No choice now, and by hurrying cross-country, we could cut closer to the car. We stumbled, fell, struggled on. The snow dragged at our feet, making it harder than running in sand. Branches whipped our faces as we dashed past threatening trees.

We hit the road. The black Trans-Am sat at the end of the driveway. If he decided to go left, we could make a dash to our car. We had a 50 percent chance. Scott scrabbled on the ground. He heaved a large slab of ice to his waist. The slab was larger than a grapefruit and had jagged edges. He hefted it carefully, then wound up and pitched it far over the waiting car. It thumped with satisfying loudness through a mass of pine branches at least fifty feet to the other side of the car. After a moment's hesitation, the Trans-Am took off in that direction.

We watched the taillights for a moment, then ran to our car and threw ourselves in. I jammed the keys into the ignition. It roared to life. The tires squealed in protest, spun on the ice, almost sank into the snow. I swore. I eased up on the gas pedal for a second, let the tires catch, then swung an arc to U-turn away from pursuit. As we circled, I saw the taillights on the other car glow bright as it braked. It began its turn. I righted the Porsche and floored it. For a few minutes, the diminishing lights of the following car pursued us; but I had the Porsche flat out. Fortunately, no one else had chosen this night for a pleasant excursion. Countless times, we plowed through growing drifts and I thought I might lose control of the car, but the tires caught the road each time and the car purred on beautifully.

At the first crossroad, I turned north. We hit Route 178 near

Rouyn. We roared back north through the sleeping town. Two miles beyond, we hit Interstate 80. For the first time, I slowed to something approaching the speed limit. I unhunched my shoulders and looked at Scott.

"Let's do that again, say sometime when we're in our nineties." He drew a deep breath. "What did you see?"

I filled him in.

Scott said, "We should tell the cops."

"What?" I said. "That we trespassed?"

"The guy followed us."

"And we followed him. We don't have a case."

He grumbled awhile. I told him that whenever we next saw Frank, I'd mention it, but I doubted they could do anything based on what had happened.

He'd tried to memorize the Trans Am's license number, too. With all the excitement and even pooling our memories, we couldn't remember any of it.

We drove the last half hour in silence. By the time we got to New Lenox, Scott's head rested on the window as he slept. I kept myself awake with thoughts of what all of it meant. I didn't feel we were close to clearing Jeff or finding out who killed Susan. Montini and Windham were hip-deep in some kind of shit—with the mystery man I'd seen tonight, I presumed. What and how I wasn't sure, but drugs were a good bet.

At home, we quickly undressed and crawled into bed. I snuggled close to Scott, draping an arm around him as he lay on his side, my chest against his back.

He yawned. I caught it and did the same. "Thanks for sticking with me," I said.

"No problem," he muttered. "One of us has to keep sane in this relationship."

I rubbed my five-o'clock shadow gently around the back of his neck.

"Shit," he said.

"I thought you liked this," I mumbled into his neck.

"I do. I forgot. Your mom called today with last-minute changes in Christmas plans."

Nigh on to perfection he may be, but besides nagging about cars, he forgets messages. I was too tired to go over that argument. We discussed familial logistics for a few minutes.

"No word from your folks?" I asked.

"Nope."

"They'll come around," I assured him. The Judy Collins tape I'd placed on the stereo clicked off. We listened to the wind, once again raised to a galelike howl. As we'd pulled up to the house, I couldn't believe how high the drifts were, three feet in some places, and this with only blowing snow from the last storm. Drowsiness and comfort crept over me.

The phone rang. "What the fuck?" I glanced at the clock. "It's one in the morning," I moaned. I plodded to the living room to pick up the phone. I'd put off getting an extension for the bedroom for ten years. As I answered the jangling thing, I could see Wolf Road out the picture window. Not a car moved on it.

7

"Mr. Mason, I'm desperate." I recognized Jeff Trask's voice.

"Where are you, Jeff?"

"In a phone booth at the gas station across from the high school."

I heard Scott pad up behind me.

"What are you doing there?"

"I can't go home. Can you help me? I'm cold."

"I'll come get you. Hold on and don't go anywhere." I hung up.

Scott asked, "Who was that and where are you going?"

Back in the bedroom, I explained as I dressed. Scott started pulling on his winter gear.

"I can go," I said. "It's only a few minutes' drive."

"No way. In this weather, even without somebody after you, it's too easy to get stuck in a drift or skid off the road." On the way out, I glanced at the thermometer hanging outside the back door. It read twenty-one below. I drove my car through eerily deserted streets. It took twenty minutes instead of the usual ten.

We saw Jeff in the phone booth, stamping his feet and pounding his arms around his chest in attempts to keep warm. We installed him in the backseat of the Chevette.

"What happened?" I asked.

"My mom bailed me out around four today. When I got home, she started in on me. When she got back from the hospital with Eric, she started in again, ranting endlessly. She wouldn't stop. Finally, I blew up. I smashed the TV in my room. I threw my stereo receiver and turntable against the wall. She tossed me out of the house. She wouldn't let me take the car."

"You should have called from home," I said.

"I tried to, but you weren't home. I tried calling all my friends for a place to stay. If parents answered, they told me no. The few kids I did talk to didn't want me at their house. I guess I have even fewer friends than I thought. Nobody wants a murder suspect around.

"So I walked to the movies and sat through *Scrooged* and *Rain Man*. But the movies closed around twelve, and you still weren't home, so I tried walking around. It was too cold. I hung around the White Hen across from school as long as I could, but I think they were getting suspicious, so I decided to give your place one last chance. You said to call anytime, Mr. Mason."

"It's okay, Jeff. We'll put you up tonight, then figure out what to do tomorrow."

"I won't go back there," he announced.

At home, I got him a few blankets and set up the couch for him. It was nearly two. Tomorrow would be soon enough for questions and answers. I did give his mother a quick call to let her know he was safe. She thanked me and agreed to the solution. She sounded grateful, relieved, and at her wits' end.

Jeff stumbled into the kitchen the next morning while I made the automatic coffee maker do its duty. Scott had brought me the simplest one on the market for my birthday. I'd managed to break three others. Machines don't like me. Or they see me coming and nudge each other and say, "Hey, Harry, here's a live one," and they break. When Scott comes into the room, they whistle innocently as if it were all my fault.

Scott entered the room and yawned good morning. He was

in jeans, a University of Arizona sweat shirt, and white socks. I wore my school clothes. Jeff had on the faded blue jeans, navy blue sweater, and gym shoes from the night before. Scott rummaged in the refrigerator. We found enough food to make an adequate breakfast.

Over last cups of coffee, Jeff said, "You're Scott Carpenter, the baseball player." Introductions the night before had gotten muddled in the cold and immediacy of the rescue.

Scott smiled and nodded.

"You live here with Mr. Mason?"

"Sometimes. I have a place of my own. Other times, he stays there with me."

"Oh," the kid said.

In my home, there's one bedroom with one king-size bed. It used to be a three-bedroom home, but I converted the other two into a one-room office-den filled with books in floor-to-ceiling bookcases and with the ultramodern electronics—computer, printer, and copier—that Scott had bought me. No other bedroom existed. The night before, Scott and I had made no secret of going to the same room. We also hadn't pranced to bed naked in front of the kid.

However, I explained briefly about us: how we'd met; how long we'd been together.

Scott said, "We're lovers." He sipped his coffee.

Jeff said, "You guys don't look gay. I mean you don't act swishy or anything. I never thought an athlete would be gay. And Mr. Mason, you said you played sports in high school and college." Toward the end of his statement, he'd begun to stumble over his words and turn red. He finished with, "I don't get it, you guys don't have earrings in your right ears."

We didn't burst out laughing at his misconceptions, and there wasn't time for a lengthy lesson on stereotypes and prejudices. I gave him a short course, but gently—to ease his embarrassment.

I asked, "How do you feel now that you know about us?"

"Okay, I guess. It's your business, not anybody else's. I still don't believe it."

"It's true," Scott said.

Silence ensued for several minutes. Finally, Jeff said, "What's going to happen today?"

"I'm going to school," I said. "You and Scott can meet me afterward."

"What about tonight?" Jeff asked.

"I'm going to talk to your dad and mom today," I said. "If either one will take you back, would you go?"

"No way. Can't I stay with you guys?"

I let it drop. I wasn't going to argue about it. During the day, I'd check with the police and maybe the social worker.

At any rate, he seemed content enough with Scott for the moment. How many kids could say they spent the day with Scott Carpenter, baseball megastar?

Outdoors, the wind had died. Bitter cold gripped the depressingly white landscape.

The announcer on WFMT, a major fine-arts station in Chicago, droned in his usual calm voice that it was twenty-three below zero, a new record. Somehow I expect that if an incredible disaster occurred, the WFMT announcer would say in the same calm drone, "The entire state of Kansas disappeared today, and in fine-arts news, a new recording of Beethoven's Ninth Symphony will be previewed during the seven-o'clock hour this evening."

For teachers, the day before Christmas vacation is perhaps the toughest day of the year, rivaled only by the last day of school. The kids are nuts, hyper, and off the wall. You'd think that by high school, the excitement of Christmas coming would have faded in their jaded minds; but no, vacations's coming and they're ready. The only ones worse than the kids are the teachers. By Christmas, we're more than set to escape.

I found my classroom door unlocked. Another rude awakening was Oliver Sandgrace perched on the edge of my desk. Who needs superintendents at seven-thirty in the morning? I'd never met him. I introduced myself. He didn't invite me to sit. I sprawled in the chair behind my desk, causing him to twist uncomfortably and finally to reseat himself.

A prissy little man in his late fifties, he has a birthmark in the middle of his bald forehead, about three inches to the left of where Mikhail Gorbachev has his, only Sandgrace's is rounder. It looks as if he's gotten sunburned on the one spot, while the rest of his head gleams pinkly. He wore a black business suit with a red tie.

He said, "Several board members have brought complaints about you, Mr. Mason."

"And why is that important?"

"We're here to serve the public. Dealing with the community is part of our job." This was delivered in a severe tone.

"I thought we were here to teach kids."

"I'm not going to argue with you, Mr. Mason, I'm telling you."

I interrupted. "Have I broken the contract, state law, or school code? Is there a problem with my performance in the classroom?"

I got a frosty "Don't interrupt me until I'm quite finished. I don't like your attitude."

"I apologize for interrupting. I don't care if you don't like my attitude."

"We may be talking about your status as a teacher in this district," he huffed.

"You threatening to fire me?" I laughed. "Let's call in the union president, then. Make your threats in front of him. I'll stack my sixteen years of excellent evaluations against anything you've got."

He got off the desk, paced the room a moment. When he resumed talking, he switched tactics. "You haven't given me a chance. Maybe I started out overly harsh. I've read those evaluations. You are a good teacher. But you're meddling in murder, for which you have no expertise or training. And you're upsetting people in the district."

"Who?"

"I'm not at liberty to say."

"Then you'll need to familiarize yourself with Article Seven, Section A, paragraph two of the current board-union contract. It says that a teacher has the right to know the name of the complainant and the nature of the complaint." Being union building rep, I'd had to read the damn contract several million times. I can quote parts of the stupid thing in my sleep.

"I don't need you to tell me what's in the contract," Sandgrace said.

"Obviously you do."

"Why are you so hostile?" he asked.

We stared at each other a moment. He broke the contact first. I watched his gray eyes dart about the room. They came back to rest on mine.

"I'm here representing the Board of Education. They are your and my bosses, whether we like it or not. They told me to tell you to cease your activities connected with Jeff Trask. Specifically, not to talk to the kids, teachers, or parents involved."

"On what authority do they make that demand?"

He looked nonplussed.

"They have no jurisdiction over my activities outside of school. I have broken neither the law, which you are in no position to enforce, nor have I violated school code, union contract, or job description."

"You can't keep harassing parents. I won't have it. If necessary, I'll talk to the police about your activities."

"Then it's the police's problem, not yours, isn't it?" I asked.

"I can't have one of my staff involved in a criminal investigation," he said.

"Is there a job-related issue here?"

"How dare you defy me? You teachers and your union are not all-powerful."

"Neither are you and the board."

He gave up trying to sound reasonable. "You realize there will be repercussions for you, Mr. Mason?"

"What will those be?" I asked.

"The board will decide at its next meeting."

"Keep your idle threats, but do remember: if necessary, the union can tie you up in hearings for years if you try harassing me."

He shook his head and left.

Administrators are such assholes. I suspected a cover-up of some kind before; now I was sure of it. I knew I'd keep digging. I'd also need to be more careful. I might sneer at Sandgrace's threats, but I didn't want to push anybody too far beyond their limits. He was just a guy doing and protecting his own job.

The instant the bell rang for lunch, Meg appeared outside my classroom door. She waited for the kids to leave. She wore a wicked grin. It usually meant somebody was in deep shit.

She closed the door and motioned me over to the windows. She looked over her shoulder.

"A little melodramatic, Meg?"

"You won't believe this. I've got hot gossip, and I mean torrid." She gave a dramatic pause. She'd studied drama in college before getting her library degree. "First, you must understand this is from an unreliable source."

"Then what good is it?"

"Listen," she said, thumping my elbow. "George Windham and Pete Montini are the major source of drugs in the school. They're part of a major drug network. I can't prove they sell directly to kids. They have students doing the actual selling. They work through intermediaries so the kids at school won't know who's behind it."

I told her what I'd heard from Eric and what George had told me without revealing my sources.

"It's true, then," she said.

I shrugged. "You say your source is unreliable. Do I believe George? He claims he's stopped, and that he only bought drugs. Certainly, I think he and Pete are up to something. At least Pete is." I told her about the chase and the house.

After numerous warnings to be careful and a reconfirmation of lunch Saturday, she left.

I phoned Mr. and Mrs. Trask. Dad said keep the kid. Mom wanted to calm down a bit yet. She asked whether we'd keep him a while longer.

After my tutoring group left, I got hold of Frank Murphy at the police station. He listened to all I told him. He said he'd check it out, but he told me whatever I had was speculative and circumstantial, although if I wanted, he'd arrest Montini for trying to run us off the road. I didn't want that for now. I let it go.

I was late for meeting Scott and Jeff, so I hurried to my classroom for my coat. They stood in the doorway.

Scott said, "Instead of letting the car run, I thought we'd meet you here."

"I'd like to talk to Paul Conlan before we go," I said. We walked down to the gym. They stayed in the hall while I stood inside the doors waiting for a pause in movement. The basketball team ran plays, shouting and calling encouragement to each other. Montini caught my eye and turned his back. With that, instead of waiting, I marched across the floor and told him I needed to see Paul. While he hesitated, I beckoned Paul over. I told the boy what I wanted. He looked to Montini for approval.

With a snarl, Pete said, "Who gives a shit?" and walked away.

In his faded orange practice uniform, dripping sweat and breathing hard, Paul followed me into the hallway. The two boys nodded coolly at each other.

"Paul," I said, "I wanted to ask a few more questions about your party."

He pointed at Jeff. "Ask him. He was there. The cops questioned me. They said I didn't do anything wrong. I'm in the clear."

Jeff said, "Come on, Paul. You've got to help me. I didn't kill Susan. Mr. Mason might be able to find who did it. Why won't you talk to him?"

"He's just a schoolteacher. He can't do anything."

"Paul, we were buddies. I need help," Jeff said. The sounds of slapping basketballs and running feet echoed around the plaintiveness of Jeff's plea.

"You may have needed my friendship," Paul said, "but I was never a buddy of yours. You hung around like a wimp. You were never really one of the guys."

"What happened since we last talked?" I asked. I would never have expected such cruelty from Paul Conlan. Whenever I'd seen him around school, he was always the big-deal athlete but with plenty of time to be generous to the adoring hordes. He'd managed to pull this off without seeming condescending or phony. Now his face showed anger and hate, and yet underneath I thought I detected a note of fear.

Paul said, "All of you stay away from me. I don't need this murder shit to screw up my chances for college and a pro career. I've got a chance to go to a top-rated school. Leave me out of this. Leave me alone."

Jeff quivered with anger. "You bastard," he said. "All the times I trusted you. All the dreams we had about our futures."

"Forget it," Paul interrupted. "That was kid stuff. I got nothing to say about the party or anything else. I have to get back to practice." He yanked open the gym door and left us.

"He's not like that," Jeff said. Tears waited at the edges of his eyes. "He didn't mean that stuff. He's scared."

"Of what?"

"I don't know," he said.

I wondered what had hardened Paul's attitude since I'd talked to him last.

Outside, the early evening was clear and very cold. No wind

blew. They predicted another record cold night. The announcer for WFMT informed us that the high temperature for the day had been seven below. We drove my Chevette because it had a backseat.

We went to my place to work out. With bits and scraps of extra weights, we found enough to set up Jeff. He got tired first and went upstairs to take a shower. Scott and I finished at the same time. While he showered, I turned on the evening news. The lead story: The Chicago City Council passed the Gay Rights Ordinance after thirteen years. I wanted to go to town and go out for at least one drink to celebrate. I mentioned it to Scott as I got dressed. We decided that it was as reasonable to have Jeff stay at Scott's apartment as it was to have him stay at my place. Jeff thought it was great. He'd get to see where the famous baseball star Scott Carpenter lived.

The passage of the Gay Rights Ordinance had the usual to do with making it as palatable as possible to the religious bigots by adding a smorgasbord of discriminated-against groups, and then tailoring it so that the religious bigots wouldn't have to obey it. And if a huge chunk of the aldermen hadn't been running for mayor in the special mayoral election, it still probably wouldn't have passed. I guess we aren't supposed to question the motives of our straight friends when they condescend to give us what should have been ours years before. Nonetheless, I'd worked on committees to get the damn thing passed, and I did feel good about it.

First, we stopped for dinner at Lawry's the Prime Rib. The amount of trouble we have with Scott's fame when we go out varies. When we first met, he was hesitant about being seen out with a guy. That much of a closet, I refused to accept. He's gotten much better about that over the years. However, as his fame has grown, so have the hassles. We go out less busy days of the week and at an hour when restaurants aren't likely to be crowded. Sometimes, we've been in the middle of vast crowds on the lakefront and haven't been recognized, and yet in the most intimate and expensive restaurants, we've been forced to leave because of obnoxious patrons. This night, because of the weather, the restaurant wasn't crowded. Except for one waitress, whom Scott signed an autograph for, we had a quiet meal.

At Lawry's, they've got three entrées on their dinner menu: thin, medium, or thick-cut prime rib. Here's a tip. Order the end cut. Eating it is almost better than sex. While we ate, Jeff satisfied more of his curiosity about the life of a professional sports player. They'd obviously already discussed a great deal during the day. Jeff returned several times to the subject of the World Series three years ago. Scott's fifth-game no-hitter was a phenomenal work of art. His seventh-game no-hitter was a thing of beauty, as well as being the highest-rated TV show ever.

After dessert and over coffee, I said, "I've got a few more questions about Sunday, Jeff."

He squirmed slightly but looked cooperative.

"First, I want to know how everybody got along with each other," I said.

"Okay. Becky pretty much runs things. She's got a mean mouth. Even Paul's a little afraid of her, I think. She makes plans for the group. If she wants to go to a movie, then we all go to a movie. If you disagree, she cuts you off, you're nothing, and the group goes along with her. Doris and Roger are basically an audience for her. Eric hung around mostly, I think, because he and Paul were teammates and sitting at home bored Eric. Paul and him are good friends."

"What about drugs and alcohol at the parties?"

"Kids drank." He did a more pronounced squirm. "And we did some drugs. Almost always pot. Once or twice, we did coke. I did a couple lines once." He stared at his hands as they smoothed the tablecloth.

"Who brought the drugs?"

"Every time I saw, it was Becky, although Paul usually rolled the joints or cut the lines."

Maybe Paul the saint had a few more flaws. I asked, "Did you ever buy any?"

"Once in a while, some of us would chip in for a little extra. Usually not, though. Nobody mentioned money much at all. We always had enough drugs. It wasn't a big deal. Nobody was an addict or anything."

Teenage whine and defensiveness had crept into his tone. I asked, "Do you know why Paul cut you off so badly today?"

"No." He shook his head miserably. "I thought he was my friend."

"He was the last one to see the two of you together. When I talked to him, I thought he might be hiding something."

Jeff defended his friend. "He's not like that. He's a good guy. I don't have a lot of close friends. I'm pretty quiet. I don't like to do stuff."

"He told me that."

"It's true. I'd rather sit home. Lots of times, Susan and me would go to her house and baby-sit her little brother and sister and watch TV. Especially lately, she wanted to go and do stuff."

"Was she different in any other way recently?"

He thought a moment. "Not that I noticed."

"About Paul, then."

He fiddled with a spoon and fork left from dinner. "We're buddies. He's a good teammate. He could get us to do better in a game even more than Coach could. Everybody likes him. He's great to be around when it's him and me and just the guys. When Becky's around, it's awful."

Scott said, "After this is over, maybe you and Paul can patch things up." Jeff nodded hopefully.

I asked, "Do you know anything about teachers buying drugs?" I mentioned several names.

"I heard they did. All of us in the group talked about it."

"Did you ever actually see them buying?"

He shook his head.

"Which ones were there rumors about?"

"The ones you said." As Eric had, he added a few younger teachers I only knew as names on faculty lists.

"Okay. Now tell me about Paul and Coach Montini."

College recruiters had been drooling all over Paul, Jeff told us. They came from all over. Paul and Coach Montini had meetings about it all the time. Montini had pushed Paul a lot this year. As Paul said in the hallway, he really had his heart set on a pro career. He wanted to get into a big school. He talked about it all the time. Paul attended summer athletic camps, did extra workouts, everything.

I didn't see how that information would help. I switched topics. "Was Susan connected with the drugs? Selling, carrying, delivering?"

"Not that I saw or knew about."

"Who would want to kill her?"

"I don't know."

Scott said, "What I don't get in this whole thing is, why isn't Becky Twitchell dead? Almost everybody hates her. Everything I've heard about her is negative. She's part of the drug connection. Why is she the center of everything yet taking none of the consequences of her behavior?"

"I don't know." Jeff shrugged. "Partly because she dates Paul, and everybody likes him. He's great, cool, fun to be around, always knows what to say or do."

At Scott's, we installed Jeff in front of the forty-inch stereo television. The kid spent most of the time while we were there with his mouth gaping open. I guess I'm used to it. Scott's place is done in several basic styles. The living room has dark wooden chairs and sofas covered with soft cushions. A bright white rug and floor-to-ceiling windows make it airy and bright. One wall has a cabinet with his three Cy Young Awards, M.V.P. trophies, a baseball autographed by the 1927 Yankees, framed newspaper clippings from the highlights of his career, and other souvenirs he's amassed over the years. The paintings on the walls at opposite ends of the room are of rural scenes, each over ten feet by ten. The one on the east wall has two youths about thirteen fishing in a quiet eddy of a river just after dawn. You can feel the haze and warmth of a summer morning and the closeness of the friendships of youth. On the west wall, two boys, perhaps fifteen years old, walk down a dirt road between fields of wheat—baseball, bat, and gloves in hand. Long shadows follow them as they move into a red-orange-gold sunset. At the far horizon there is a glimpse of a summer storm.

In the electronics room, where we left Jeff, were stereos, CD players, tape players, Nintendo games, computers, printers. If it existed electronically, it was probably in this room. Scott had filled the room with reclining chairs, easy chairs, bean-bag chairs, and rocking chairs.

First, we stopped to see Neil. He muttered and swore at great length. He'd been working for the Gay Rights Ordinance since 1972, when it was less than a twinkle in a queen's dream. He wanted to be out partying and celebrating. The doctor wouldn't let him leave for another day or two. His cronies from the local gay organizations had been by to cheer him up but had left to pursue more convivial surroundings. He groused at the lack of liquor. I pulled a champagne bottle from beneath my coat.

"I thought this might be necessary," I said, and presented it to him. We drank a glass or two with him. Scott promised to return with him after Christmas to visit the people with AIDS in the hospital. Early on, Scott had added visiting people with AIDS in hospitals to his schedule. Scott's done a huge number of benefits for all kinds of hospital groups. He brings in the crowds. His first priority nowadays are the requests that come in for AIDS benefits.

An hour later, we lounged comfortably in Bruce's Halfway There Bar, our hands wrapped around cups of hot coffee. It was too cold for beer. We'd left an unhappy Neil to his TV set.

Bruce's was a quiet gay bar, one of the few Scott felt comfortable in. It sat between two aged apartment buildings on

North Avenue, a block west of Wells Street. Housed in a building that might have been built the day after the Chicago fire, its main virtues were quiet and discretion. Inside, Scott was unlikely to be recognized, or if he was, the gray-suited clientele was far too discreet to notice. In this bar, even the screaming queens became whispering princesses. It was also only a short walk from there to his place.

On the left as you walked in, a wooden bar stained dark brown backed by a wall of mirrors ran the length of the room. On the right, tall black booths marched somberly to the back, interrupted by a usually silent jukebox.

Few other customers had braved the bitter cold to celebrate the passage of the ordinance. Ed, the bartender, joined us in the back booth.

"I like sitting with you guys. People think I can still date hunky men." Ed is a Chicago cop. He's around fifty, with a potbelly. He moonlights two or three nights a week as a bartender. His lover is a hairdresser named Prentice.

Briefly, we told him about the murder at school. He took a cop's cool interest but had no solutions. When we mentioned being followed, he shook his head and said, "You've got to be careful, and not just with suburban dangers. You've got to watch out for fag bashers around here."

Scott filled him in about the attack on Neil, then asked, "You had trouble with fag bashers lately?"

Ed moaned. "Last week, we had a couple guys beat up not ten feet from the door."

Used to be gay-bashing season was only in the summer. Mix those TV hate evangelists with AIDS, however, and it's become open season all year round.

Ed continued: "I'll use a gun on those bastards, if they ever get near me. Goddamn straight kids in their big brave groups attacking one or two guys. I'd like to see how brave they are with a gun in their faces."

Ed's an okay guy. I share his anger and frustration at fag bashers. I firmly believe that if more gays pressed charges and took the attackers to court, we'd all be better off.

Two new customers entered. Ed left to minister to them.

We talked of next day's schedules. Scott had a breakfast speech to give for a children's Christmas charity at the Hyatt Regency downtown. I wanted to talk to Frank Murphy to see whether what we'd learned had been helpful to them, and if they'd found out any more. I had to do some last-minute Christmas shopping, which Scott pointed out I could have done weeks ago. We finished our coffee and left. Outside, the wind had picked up again, and light snow fell. They expected the temperature to rise before morning. For now, it felt as if it were still twenty below.

At the bottom of the steps, we turned right to go east on North Avenue.

"Fucking faggots," a voice screamed. I turned to check the direction of attack. Four men weaved toward us from the west, maybe twenty feet down the sidewalk.

As we turned to face them, Scott stepped on a patch of ice. His arms flailed the air for a moment. I grabbed for him, managed to keep a firm footing, and righted us. Scott and I could handle most attackers. Jungle training helped me, and Scott was a tough fighter from way back.

"Look at the fairies." The loud one minced his words. He stopped his drunken weaving and switched from entertaining his friends to confronting us. The leader might have been twenty; the others were about the same age. We had two apiece. The fight was quite brief. One of mine lay moaning in the snow clutching a bleeding, and I hoped broken, nose. Two others ran off. Scott knelt over the last one, fist raised. "Shit," he said.

I joined him. The man on the ground stared up at him.

"Hello, Scott, faggot."

Scott didn't plaster the guy's face into oblivion at the insult. Instead, he climbed to his feet and brushed snow off himself.

The other guy, the former group leader, stood and wobbled. He inched a few steps away but didn't run.

"Who is it?" I asked.

Scott said nothing. The guy gave a nasty laugh. "I'm Jack Frampton. And the high and mighty Scott Carpenter is a fucking queer."

"Let's go," Scott said.

"We've got to turn these guys in," I said.

"We're leaving," Scott said. He began walking away.

"Better follow your lover, honey," Frampton trilled. I considered pounding his face into the snow, thought better of it, then hurried after Scott. I'd never met any of Scott's teammates until that moment. As he stomped through the biting cold and gathering snow, Scott neither looked at me nor spoke. He slammed his way into the penthouse. One light burned above the kitchen sink. I checked on Jeff. He'd gone to bed where I'd shown him in one of the spare bedrooms. He didn't stir when I opened the door. In our bedroom, Scott threw his keys against the wall. His coat, scarf, hat, and gloves followed in rapid succession. More slowly, I hung my paraphernalia on hooks and hangers.

If one of us loses his temper, it's usually me. When I do, it's volcanic. He knows the tricks to calming me down. In the press, he's often referred to as "The Ice Man." His reaction now wasn't all that odd, however. Coming out for gay people is a process, not a one-time event. Some days you feel free, open, and ready to piss on the world if they care what you do in bed. On other days, even if you've been out to yourself and others, you're ready to hide in the darkest closet—because sometimes it is safer, easier, and more secure to hide. If you're partly out, this schizophrenia can be exacerbated, and if your job is public or sensitive, it can drive you crazy. Scott's been in enough headlines to make the most wily politician envious.

Scott stomped out of the bedroom. I found him in the southwest corner of the living room. Chicago lay sprawled beyond the windows in its vast glittering array.

"Let's talk about it," I said. I touched his shoulder.

He flinched away. He stared out the window, his back to me. He rested his hand on the floor-to-ceiling window, placed his forehead next to his hand.

Early in our relationship, he'd close himself off from me in emotional situations. He'd changed and it'd become easier, but times like now could occur and talking could be tough.

I let the silence build.

Finally, he said, "I can't do what you want. I can't be open about being gay. I try. I'm thirty-seven years old, and only two months ago, I told my parents why I'm never going to bring home bouncy cute grandkids and the girl of their dreams. It's too scary for me."

"It's that way for me sometimes, too," I said.

He talked on as if I hadn't spoken.

"We live quietly. We don't shove our relationship on others. I know my closet will never be so severe that it would endanger our relationship. But now this bastard Frampton. Everything's fine for years. I'm getting better with being public. This morning with the kid, I felt good and proud. Now one asshole teammate sees me leave a gay bar and I panic."

"Maybe he won't tell."

He finally turned to me. "Don't you understand? I don't want to live in a world where I have to worry about who might tell. Who might see. Who might say. Who might start a rumor. Or worse, at which press conference after a game, which reporter will ask the question 'Do you fuck guys?' I'm fed up with living in fear. In your teaching, you don't think about it. You've got the confidence to cope. I don't." He walked partway along the glass wall to the table where he kept his World Series awards.

"You were ready to take me to your teammates' New Year's Eve gathering."

"That was a party, not a blatant announcement."

I didn't move from my spot. "You know, I do understand," I said. This wasn't the first time we'd had this type of discussion.

But then he'd never been seen in a possible compromising position by a teammate. "Do you want to try to talk to Frampton?"

"I don't want to have to talk to anybody."

"What do you want to do?" I moved toward him.

"Run. Hide. Turn the clock back to make it never have happened. Make myself not gay."

We hadn't turned the lights on. We faced each other in the glow from the city below. His blue eyes glistened almost black.

"They can make us hate ourselves so easily," I said.

"I don't hate myself."

"Every time one of us wishes we weren't gay, they've taken another step toward repressing us. We can't let that happen."

"I can't be as politically perfect as you want," he said. "I'm just a guy with a life I want to be happy about." A glint of a tear shone on his right cheek. He shook his head. "I know I'm probably making a fool out of myself. I know I could quit baseball today, and if all my endorsements ended tomorrow, even then I'd barely notice a dent in my lifestyle. I've got advantages and possibilities most gays only dream about."

I said, "The point is, you don't want to live in fear. You don't want to alter your life because you're gay. And each alteration we make for that reason diminishes us as a person. And if you had to quit because you're gay, it would hurt. You love baseball. It's been your life since you were eleven years old."

Scott said, "And when I leave, I want it to be on my terms, not because a snotty little bigot who can barely hit a major-league curve has a fucking big mouth."

I moved close to him, gripped his forearms. I felt the muscles ripple beneath my touch. I said, "You can't control what Frampton says or does. I know of no reason why any gay person need live in fear in this day and age. All of us in some way, you and I in particular when we went for the test, have had to face AIDS and the fact of our own mortality. We were lucky. We both tested negative."

His shoulders sagged. His eyes searched mine. "It never stops, does it?" he asked.

"No. It never stops," I confirmed. I pulled him close and held him tight. After a moment, I felt his arms entwine around me.

Returning from the bathroom early the next morning, I let one eye open to observe the swirling snow. I breathed a prayer of thanks to the god who gives teachers vacations. I rolled close to Scott's warmth and snuggled down to a cold winter's doze. I awoke again at seven. Scott adjusted his tie in front of the mirror.

"Go back to sleep," he said.

"What time'll you be home?" I mumbled.

"Around eleven." I watched him don his suit coat and overcoat. He stopped on my side of the bed, leaned down, and kissed me lightly on the forehead.

Jeff got up a few minutes after I did—around eight. We put together some clean clothes for him—a pair of Scott's old jeans and a flannel shirt of mine. I found enough food for a sufficient breakfast. I lazed about the apartment. Jeff tried a few of the weights in Scott's half gym, switched on the TV, wandered around restlessly through rooms. Almost shyly, he asked whether he could go out and walk around. It wasn't far to the Michigan Avenue shops. I told him it was okay but to be back soon.

I read some of McPherson's *Battle Cry of Freedom*. Around ten, I decided on a shower. After I was done, dripping wet, still toweling my hair, I heard the buzz from the doorman twenty stories below. I presumed it was Jeff.

Instead, the doorman's voice said, "A Mr. Courtland for you, sir."

A voice bellowed in the distance, "I'll be up in a second."

The doorman uttered a protest. The phone on the other end clicked off.

Doug Courtland was Scott's best friend on the team. Scott

described him as a six-foot-six chunk of first baseman. They elected him team captain and player union rep, both tributes to his popularity and shrewdness. He often tried hiding behind a "dumb hick from Arkansas" facade. They shared a rural southern background and an affinity for late-night poker on the road. It was his party we planned to attend New Year's Eve.

Towel draped around my neck and wearing the bottom to a warm-up suit, I padded to the door to answer his ring.

He gave me this big goofy grin when he saw me. "You're Tom, right?" He had one fist gripped on to a very red and angry Jack Frampton.

I invited them in.

"Scott's mentioned you a few times." Courtland filled a large portion of the entryway.

"Scott's not home," I said.

Frampton growled something unintelligible.

"I know he's not home," Courtland said. "He's giving a talk. I saw it on the club's press schedule."

"Oh," I said. I put some coffee on, stepped into the bedroom, threw on some jeans, socks, and a sweat shirt, and joined them in the kitchen. The breakfast nook where we sat overlooks Lake Michigan. I poured coffee.

Courtland said, "I got a call early this morning from this jerk." He pointed a thumb at Frampton. "I hear you met last night. Jack is quite concerned about your relationship with my best friend. I wish Scott felt free enough to tell me about you. I guessed he was gay years ago. I figured he never brought it up, so it wasn't my business. It never stopped our friendship, so I ignored it."

I wasn't sure what to say.

"I stopped here for three reasons. To have Jack apologize, to meet you, the person my best friend loves, and to invite you both over for dinner next week. My wife and I would love to have you."

My simple thanks seemed inadequate.

"From Frampton's call, I figured you guys must be staying in town. I knew you were a schoolteacher from what Scott had said."

"What else did he say about me?"

"Not much." He grinned. "He's very discreet, but you can't fool a real friend when you're in love. I guessed you might be off from school, so I thought I might come over."

It turned out Frampton had called Courtland with the news first thing. He and his buddies had been carousing in various watering holes on Wells Street before they'd run into us. They'd attacked gays outside Bruce's before. This time, they'd got more than they'd bargained for. Frampton had thought Courtland would join him in universal outrage and condemnation of Scott. Mistake.

We talked until the front door opened. Scott entered the kitchen a minute later. He observed the sullen Frampton staring out the window at one end of the room while Doug and I sat at the kitchen table.

"Come here, you." Courtland motioned Frampton over. "You got something to say to these guys, say it to their faces, not some sneaking coward bullshit." Courtland glowered.

"I'm sorry about last night." Frampton mumbled the apology. His brashness showed briefly. "I still don't like faggots."

Courtland grabbed him. "Who don't you like?"

Frampton cast a guilty look at all three of us. "Gay people," he muttered.

Courtland slapped him on the ass. "Good boy. There's hope for you yet. You're honest and you can learn."

Scott said, "Jack, if you'd like to talk about it sometime or ask questions . . ."

"I guess I'd like to leave it alone for now," Frampton said.

Scott offered him his hand. The kid looked surprised. He shook hands almost gratefully.

"I'd like to go," Frampton said.

After he left, Courtland said, "You should have told me."

"I was scared," Scott said. "But what about Frampton?"

Courtland smiled. "Nothing about him. Let him talk. You're the best right-hand pitcher in baseball. What's to care? Besides, if he tells, you turn him in for assault. I already explained that to him."

I pushed for turning Frampton in, but they convinced me he'd learned a lesson. Before Doug left, we agreed to be at his house the next Friday for dinner.

A half hour later, a rosy-cheeked Jeff strolled into the penthouse. We decided to do the last-minute Christmas shopping at Water Tower Place.

In the bedroom as we changed, I said, "Courtland's nice, funny. How do you feel about him coming here?"

"Stunned when I saw you guys. Great now that it's over."

We took Jeff with us. Outside, the wind roared in off the Lake, the sun flaring off the winter whiteness. After twelve hours of steadily rising temperatures, it was all of five above. The prediction was for well below zero again by nightfall, another arctic blast marching in from Canada. The northeast wind pushed gray clouds in from Lake Michigan. The Lake level had fallen the past year, but at some points, waves still crashed high against the shore, spraying water over vulnerable sections of Lake Shore Drive.

We pulled off onto Michigan Avenue. It's hard to buy Christmas gifts for Scott, he being a fabulously wealthy millionaire. We get each other surprise gifts each year. I knew he'd never guess this year's. I picked up my father's shirts at Field's. Mom said he needed several. She usually has the lowdown on who needs what in the family. Scott and I give my nieces and nephews some of the best toys in the universe. We go equal shares on that.

We dumped the gifts at Scott's. I looked forward to a quiet leisurely afternoon. The phone rang. Scott picked it up in the kitchen. A minute later, he entered the living room, his face pale.

"What's wrong?" I asked.

"That was Frank Murphy at the River's Edge police station. Roger Daniels is dead."

"Did Murphy say what happened?"

"No. He wants to see us."

I told Jeff. "He can't be dead," was his stunned response. "He was my friend. Next to Paul, my best friend at school."

8

We drove to the River's Edge police station. As usual, a lone cop sat behind the counter. She directed us to one of the interrogation rooms.

We left Jeff in an out-of-the-way office, with a cup of hot chocolate. Frank had met Scott before. Murphy got us settled, then said, "This is pure hell."

He told us they'd found Roger's body under the radio tower just east of La Grange Road near Tinley Gardens. Some kids were snowmobiling and found him. Somebody'd shot him gangland style—handcuffed, with a bullet through the back of his head.

"Why kill him?" I asked.

"We don't know that. All we do know is he died somewhere else. The killer or killers dumped his body there."

I thought about how long Jeff had been gone that morning. Maybe a little over two hours. I dismissed the possibility. Not enough time and no transportation.

"You guys found anything new?" he asked.

I told him about Jeff's information the night before. When I finished, he shook his head. He sipped coffee from a Styrofoam cup, and mumbled a curse. "Can't see where that will help. The drug stuff may give us a connection, but I doubt it. Susan and Roger were fringe players, if that much, in any kind of drug scheme. We haven't found any such connection. I honestly don't think it has anything to do with the murder. I don't doubt you've uncovered something nastily illegal. Although except for the car tag you've played, you've witnessed nothing criminal."

I started to protest. He held up a hand. "Wait. You keep implicating this Becky Twitchell, but we haven't been able to connect her to anything. She claims she never talked to Jeff at all about any threats."

He stood up, walked around the room, kicked a table leg. He sighed. "What I've done is called all the parents and school officials together. I'll be meeting with them in a few minutes. The first thing we'll probably do is put cops in the high school for a while after vacation."

"But the attacks weren't at school," Scott said.

"No, but there's too much coincidence involved. Plus, I've had your superintendent on the phone three times today demanding extra protection. It probably won't do any good, but the community will see a real cop, so they may think we're doing something."

"It'll shut a few people up," I said.

"I hope. Second, I want you to be there when I meet with these people, unofficially, of course. We're setting up a task force. We've got to deal with the parents' and the community's fears. In fifteen minutes, I've got to cope with them. I'd like you both there if you're willing. You've found some information that may turn out to be useful."

In the basement meeting room, bare pipes dripped cool water onto us. Two naked light bulbs glared overhead. Three metal couches with rummage-sale reject cushions sat against the walls. It was the kind of place where they used to torture prisoners in 1930s gangster movies. Frank introduced us to anyone we didn't know.

Carolyn Blackburn and Oliver Sandgrace sat on the couch directly opposite the door. The Twitchells filled another. Mrs. Conlan and Mrs. Bradford sat on the third couch. Their husbands grouped themselves on metal folding chairs near the exit. Roger's parents, the Danielses, stood in a far corner of the room, looking dazed and forlorn. In the corner across from them sat the Warrens, Susan's parents. Mrs. Trask stood behind the Twitchells. Mr. Trask came in right behind us and stayed near the men at the door, the farthest point from his wife he could get.

The parents all talked at Murphy as soon as they saw him. Anxious queries turned to muttered anger when some of them saw Mr. Trask and me.

"He doesn't belong here." Sandgrace pointed at me.

Mrs. Twitchell pointed to Mr. and Mrs. Trask. "I don't want the parents of a killer in here."

Chaos ensued. Parents shouted; administrators and board members argued. Those who hadn't met Scott spent some time being awed by his presence. Parental concern quickly returned, however, and they went back to attacking Frank.

Scott and I remained to the left of the doorway. Murphy took an old lead pipe and bashed it against a radiator. It clanged resoundingly. They all shut up.

"Now," Frank said. "You're all here by invitation of the police. We've got a dangerous situation. Someone has killed two children in this community and badly beaten another. We have mobilized city, county, and state task forces to deal with this problem."

"Forget this task-force nonsense," Mrs. Twitchell said. "Why are you bothering our children with accusations? What are you doing to catch the killer and protect our kids? When are you going to stop harassing us, and stop those two from causing trouble?" She waved bright orange fingernails at us. Her nails clashed horribly with her fluorescent blue skirt and tangerine-colored blouse. The blouse was sheer and tight, showing off her considerable endowments for anybody to appreciate.

Frank sighed audibly. "Everything humanly possible is being done, including calling you all here. If some of you object to others, you'll have to ignore it for now. We need everybody's help. The murders and the beating seem to revolve around the kids who were at last Sunday's party at the Conlans'. The key is there."

Parents erupted angrily. Finally, Mrs. Twitchell's voice prevailed. "How dare you imply one of our children murdered these two!"

Murphy spoke through clenched teeth. "Mrs. Twitchell, and the rest of you, please! I am not implying your kids are murderers. I think we need to be concerned about why two children from this group are dead. Another has been attacked and only saved by Mr. Mason and Mr. Carpenter. If there is some connection, we need to find it. In addition, we need to take precautions in case someone has singled out these kids for whatever reason. The school personnel are here so we can work out some strategies to keep the situation from getting beyond these two. I think we need to coordinate our efforts."

Most parental and administrative heads nodded.

"What about Jeff Trask?" Mrs. Twitchell asked. "Isn't he your prime suspect?

"He was and is, for Susan's murder. But he has an alibi for Roger's. We need to cover any other bases in case we're wrong in suspecting him in the first murder."

"Why attack these kids?" Mr. Bradford asked.

"That's what I hope we can work on," Murphy said. For an hour, the parents discussed their kids. They added nothing to what Scott and I already knew. Their ignorance, illusions, or delusions about their children were profound. If I didn't know the kids personally, I doubt if I'd have recognized them from their parents' descriptions. The parents straggled out of the meeting. Most expressed anger and doubts about what had been or could be done.

A somewhat repentant Jeff left with his mother.

Oliver Sandgrace, Harry Conlan, and Mrs. Twitchell cornered Murphy after the other parents had left. "Mr. Mason has been talking to parents and children, upsetting everyone. I'm sure the police disapprove of this, as I've already mentioned," Mrs. Twitchell said. "I want to know what you intend to do about it."

Murphy faced her. He said, "I'm not sure I understand the problem. Perhaps you could tell me exactly what it is you want."

Mrs. Twitchell's smug look joined the tone of her voice as she said, "Mason has bothered people." She tugged her pink calf-length down coat closer around her shoulders. "There have been complaints. I know the school board doesn't like it. He has to stop."

Frank said, "Mrs. Twitchell, I suggest you leave the decision on what people can or cannot do in a homicide investigation in the hands of the police. If Mr. Mason is a problem at school, then you can deal with it any way you want. Here, I make the decisions."

"Maybe you don't understand," Mrs. Twitchell said. "We're taxpayers and we're demanding you take action. We can go to your superiors, you know."

"If you want to talk to my boss, his secretary is down the hall."

Mrs. Twitchell swung on the other two. "Well," she demanded, "say something." But they said little and did less. I wasn't their biggest problem. Someone was killing their kids. They had to do something about that. They left. Frank warned us to be careful and to call him immediately if there was danger or any problem.

The Danielses and Bradfords met us in front of the admitting desk. They wanted to talk. The cop on duty led us to the same interrogation room as on Monday night.

In the dreary room, I spoke words of comfort and regret to the Danielses. Mrs. Daniels, eyes red-rimmed from weeping but voice firm, said, "Mr. Mason, you were a great help to Roger when he was a freshman. We want your assistance now. We want to know why Roger died and who killed him."

Mr. Daniels added, "We want more than the police. They're good at platitudes, but that's not good enough. This is our son. We need answers."

The Bradfords, both short and tubby, expressed fear for their daughter's safety. "We appreciate your concern, despite what the board members said," Mr. Bradford said.

Mrs. Bradford harrumphed, "Sally Twitchell is a social-climbing bitch. She thinks she's got power over people because she's head of that silly school board. They haven't made a sane decision in years."

"How's Doris been taking all this?" I asked.

Mr. Bradford said, "That's the funny part. She acts cool and disdainful, as if it didn't touch her. As if she didn't care. Maybe she wasn't best friends with Susan, but she dated Roger occasionally, and now it's as if neither of them ever existed."

Mrs. Bradford said, "We've tried to talk to her about it, without the least success. I think it's because she's so frightened, and we don't know why."

"Do you have any idea why Roger died?" I asked the Danielses.

"No," Mr. Daniels said. "He acted so different lately. This week, he stayed in his room, door shut, earphones clamped to his head. He took no interest in anything. We tried ignoring it at first, then we tried talking to him. Nothing worked."

"Somebody murdered our son," Mrs. Daniels said. "We want that person caught and punished. As we said, we want your help. We have confidence in you. We know you."

"What have the police told you so far?" I asked.

"Beyond the facts on finding him, almost nothing," Mrs. Daniels said.

We got a brief litany of suspicions about Becky Twitchell and another earful about her evil ways.

We talked awhile longer, but they had no further information. We promised to do what we could.

* * *

Outside, the sun had broken through the murky gloom of the late December day. It must have been nearly twenty degrees above zero. All the streets were clear. The drifts at the roadsides had begun their change from light gray to black encrusted.

The radio announcer predicted a 60 percent possibility of snow.

In the car, Scott said, "I am beginning to dread the name Becky Twitchell."

"You should meet her up close and personal. Then you could truly dislike her."

"How about if I get to meet her, instead of saying hello, I puke all over her?" Scott asked.

"Certainly an appropriate response." I added, "Each set of parents has experienced increased negative feelings from or with their kids since the first murder."

"The kids know who the murderer is and they're concealing it?" Scott asked. "Maybe Becky's the killer and she's got something on each one of them, including the adults, that can keep them quiet."

I said, "Becky may be the world's most completely evil human being since Adolf Hitler, but I don't think she's capable on her own of causing all that's happened. She'd have to have some motivation to kill Susan. She'd have to have been able to attack and almost kill Eric, and drag him around the school on her own. The same for murdering Roger."

"So she had an accomplice."

"Certainly there are at least two in on this. I suspect more. My guess is the drugs and murders are connected. We simply have to find what the connection is. To me, the most obvious reason we're being hassled is that we're stepping on the toes of the drug crowd as we work on the murders."

"If the drugs and murders are connected," Scott said, "then the teachers are involved in the murders."

I'd thought of that. We talked as I cruised toward Wolf Road on 159th Street. Scott tapped his coat-sleeve buttons on the side window. He said, "Could kids really keep the identity of a killer secret?"

"Maybe."

In the next five minutes, he managed to ask all the exasperating questions that had been nagging at me. How did George and Pete get involved in the drugs and why? Who supplied them? Were they really in league with Becky? What possible reason could either of them have for killing Susan? No one we'd talked to said she was involved in the drug scene, or connected in any significant way to the adults involved.

I responded to his catechizing with some asperity. "I hope you don't think this is remarkable, but I don't know the answer to your questions. You're badgering me with impossible questions. I'm trying my damnedest."

"Sorry." His deep voice thrummed soothingly. "I guess I got overzealous."

" 'S okay," I mumbled. I handed him the master list of names and addresses of those involved in the murder. "Here, make yourself useful. Navigate us to Mr. Trask's." We hadn't been able to catch him after the meeting, and I wanted to talk to him.

We twisted through the streets of several subdivisions before we got to his house. This was the oldest section of River's Edge. The trees that lined the streets were gray giants that promised vast comfort and restfulness on long summer days. We found a cul-de-sac surrounded by crumbling homes. The oldest, dingiest, and dirtiest was the one we wanted. The roof of the boxy rectangle had tar paper showing. The north wall of the garage had caved in. A battered Ford pickup truck sagged in the driveway. Old tires half-covered with snow rested in scattered patterns on the lawn. In the middle of these mounds of rubber, broken bits of bricks sat in a pile half-covered with a torn tarp that flapped in the wind. The snow we'd had couldn't conceal the rank ugliness and squalor of Mr. Trask's home.

He met us at the door with a Strohs beer in one hand, a bag of Dorritos in the other, and a gut in between that had to be the result of years of indulging in the first two.

He squinted at us through the storm door. I had to bellow to be heard over a television set. I got a suspicious look, but he opened the door.

He marched us into the living room. Plastic covered the windows, a form of ersatz insulation for the less-well-put-together home. A double-sized lounge chair sat squarely in front of a TV, which blared a football game at us. They were the only pieces of furniture in the room. He lowered the decibel of the TV. An open ice chest crammed with beer cans and next to it a pyramid of unopened Dorrito bags showed preparation for a long winter's day glued to the TV. A mold-encrusted sandwich peeked from under the chair, testifying that some of the trash had arrived prior to now. A dark blue and orange Bears shirt draped over his stomach and hung halfway to his thighs. Faded jeans and shower clogs finished the outfit.

Trask said, "Wait until the guys on the second shift hear this. Scott Carpenter in my home. Can I shake your hand?"

Trask stared at his hand after they accomplished this feat. "Damn, I've touched the most famous right arm in America." He got misty-eyed.

Scott said, "I wished we'd had more time to talk earlier."

He grinned at us impishly. "That shit Twitchell and those stupid administrators grabbed me at the police station. They're as worthless as the cops. They tried to warn me about talking to you guys. I think that Mrs. Twitchell is hot-looking for an old broad. But she's stupid. It's her I'd never talk to. She's a bigger bitch than my wife."

He grabbed some of the older-looking bits of debris and led us to a tiny kitchen, all torn lace and faded plastic flowers. He dumped his trash near enough to the garbage can and invited us to sit at the kitchen table. "Jesus, Scott Carpenter in my kitchen. They told me you were bad guys and to keep you out."

He pointed to me. "I thought you were kind of a shit at the police station the other night." He belched loudly. "But you know Scott Carpenter. Shit." He looked from one to the other of us. He scratched his stomach and squinted at us. "Are you bad guys?"

"The worst," I said. "Mrs. Twitchell hates us."

"But my wife likes you. Can't talk enough about what you did for the kids in teaching them. Though she's probably right about that. I haven't been able to get anything through their thick skulls." He switched topics abruptly. "My wife always tries to act better than herself. She's the one who wanted the divorce. Old, fat Jerome Horatio Trask who couldn't see over his gut to his prick wasn't good enough for her." He guzzled half a beer, excused himself profusely for his rudeness, and without asking plunked two cold cans of Strohs in front of us. We popped the tops and joined him.

"I know those people laugh at me behind my back. I don't care. What can I do for you two?"

"We're trying to find out who killed the kids."

"My ex-wife didn't do it. She's too worried about being clean and neat. Everything has to be perfect for her. I was fifteen years ago." He patted his gut. "I had a washboard stomach and could fuck for hours. To hell with her."

"We didn't suspect your wife," I said.

"No, huh? Too bad. If she'd done it, I might get to see the kids more often." He drank.

"We need some information," Scott said.

"No problem. You want to know what my idiot son has been up to." He shook his head sadly. "I honestly don't know."

For a moment, I thought elements of total sobriety existed in that statement.

He drank. "But what the fuck, kids are kids, you know. They grow up. They move out. My boys aren't the brightest, but if they weren't so goddamn lazy, they could make something out of themselves. It's all my ex-wife's fault. She coddles the little bastards. Boys need to get straightened out by someone they fear."

He went on to propound his philosophy of child rearing, a sort of mixture of Rambo and Attila the Hun.

After another solid snort of beer, he switched topics again. "Now, these parents are strange. The Twitchells and the Conlans. They don't like you. They don't want me talking to you, threatened me in fact." He roared with laughter. "Stupid fuckers!"

"Why not talk to us?" Scott asked.

"Beats the living shit out of me! Those rich assholes think they run everything, and when something blows up in their stupid faces, they try to cover everything up. My kids'll get screwed if they've got anything to do with it. They underestimate Jerome Horatio Trask." He rolled a muscle or two in his arms. It resembled someone moving reserves of old fat from waste-storage locations. "I wrestled in high school. Almost went to the state championships one year." He sighed wistfully and got dewy-eyed.

"What happened?" Scott asked.

"I got a girl pregnant. Everything got fucked up. I almost didn't even graduate. Barely escaped marrying the bitch. The bastard parents were well connected. All those fat cats have it in for us working stiffs." He ranted on about the evil capitalist bosses for a few minutes.

I got him back on track by asking whether anything else unusual had happened since Susan's murder.

"One thing. One of those coaches from school called for Eric. They never call here. They don't like me. Just because I go to the games and cheer for my boys. Those assholes don't know shit about coaching, and they don't like to hear it from somebody who knows what they're doing."

I tried to get the name of who had called. But try as I could to jog his memory, it was lost among the Dorritos and beer already crammed there. As we moved to the door to leave,

Trask said, "How'd you throw that second no-hitter in the Series?"

"Skillfully and carefully," Scott said.

An echo of laughter rolled around the room. Trask said, "I'll never forget watching it. No-hitter in game five, then bing, no-hitter in game seven. Let me shake your hand again." This accomplished, he stared at his hand again.

In the car, "We believe this one?" Scott said.

"Maybe. I want to talk to friendly Harry Conlan and find out why he joined in the group to stop us."

We arrived at the Conlans' a few minutes later. Only Paul was home. Mom and Dad were out doing last-minute Christmas shopping. He was too polite not to let us in, but we remained standing in the front hallway.

"Tell me your connection with Becky's drug schemes," I said.

He paled and looked close to tears.

"Go easy, Tom," Scott said. He turned to Paul. "Can we sit and talk quietly for a few minutes?"

Paul shook his head no, but we led him to the room where we'd talked to the Conlans earlier in the week. Paul paced the room as we sat. I tried asking questions. For several minutes, he wouldn't answer.

Scott asked, "Is it that bad?"

"I can't talk to you guys." Paul stopped in front of the couch where we sat. He held out his arms pleading. "I want a pro career." He closed his fists. "I'm so close. I can't get thrown out of sports. Maybe I did some stupid stuff, but it can be taken care of. My dad says everything's going to be fine. But you two keep stirring things up. And now Roger's dead. I'm afraid I'll be next, or one of my other friends. Don't you understand? Two people I knew are dead. They say Jeff's got an alibi for one. I guess that's true, but, maybe he's nuts."

"Paul." I said his name softly. He stopped. I repeated his name, then said, "Obviously you're in the middle of something that's way over your head. Tell us and we'll help."

"I can't," he whispered. "They'll kill me, too."

"Who will?" I asked.

He stumbled to the French windows and stared at the expanse of whiteness that stretched to the fields beyond. He leaned his head against the glass. I saw a cloud of mist form on the cold pane from his labored breathing.

"Please leave," he said.

"Paul, if you know who killed Susan and Roger, you've got to tell us. If you're in danger, tell someone, your mom and dad, the police, Coach Montini. You can't hold all this in."

"I can't tell you anything. I don't know anything," he said dully.

"You just said—" I began.

"Well, forget what I just said. It's nothing you or anybody else can do anything about."

"At least let us try," I said.

Something snapped in him. He turned to us, raging. "You think you understand so goddamn much. Some smartass teacher playing detective. You can't figure out anything. You're so stupid. You're such shit." Tears and sobs mingled with his shouts. "Get out. You're in as much danger as anybody. Get out and leave me alone."

"Yes, you'd better go."

We whirled to the doorway. Mr. Conlan strode toward us. Mrs. Conlan stood behind him.

"Leave my home," he said.

"Not until I find out why your son is so frightened."

"My son needs you to leave."

"Don't you care about what's destroying your boy?"

"You are. You've disturbed this family too long." He reached out to touch his son. The boy knocked the arm aside and fled. Mr. Conlan said, "Sylvia, call the police." She marched to the coffee table, picked up the phone, and punched three numbers.

Our movements to exit at this point were slow enough to

salvage some dignity but quick enough to cause her to drop the receiver.

It was three. We decided to try Susan's parents. The funeral had been the day before. I thought they might be at home. I didn't know how much they'd welcome our presence or our questions, but we had to try. I needed to know more about Susan.

We rode through quiet streets lined with massive naked trees. The Warrens lived in the Wheatfield Forest subdivision. The homes were among the oldest and smallest in the area. An elderly man answered the door. I explained that we wanted to talk to the Warrens. He seemed uncertain, but after a moment's hesitation let us in and led us into the living room. Five minutes passed before the Warrens joined us. Mr. Warren wore a gray suit. His wife had on a severe black dress and white blouse. An open Bible, red bookmark ribbon slashed across the open page, gleamed in the middle of an oaken coffee table. They sat down. Mr. Warren rested his elbows on his knees. Greasy oil held his hair plastered to his head. Mrs. Warren crossed her legs at the ankle and stared anxiously forward.

I expressed my condolences. Mrs. Warren gave a weak smile of appreciation. I talked about helping Jeff and wanting to learn all I could about his relationship with Susan. I finished my explanation. "We're trying to find the murderer. Can you tell us anything of her life in the past few weeks? Had she changed any? Said anything? Any obvious problems?"

Mrs. Warren answered, "She was the same as she'd always been. All three of us attended services Sunday mornings and Wednesday evenings. We prayed together at every meal."

Mr. Warren added, "She never complained, never appeared troubled."

"She was a good girl." Mrs. Warren unclasped her hands, smoothed her dress, and continued. "She'd escaped so many of the silly traumas of most adolescents."

"Jeff said you sent them to a family-planning clinic."

Mr. Warren looked confused. Mrs. Warren clutched her throat guiltily. She said, "I never told you, Allan." She patted his arm. "I knew you'd be angry." She turned to us. "Our daughter was a good girl. But I am a realistic woman. She told me they weren't doing anything, but I insisted she go."

Mr. Warren patted his wife's hand. "You did what you thought was best," he said.

"Could you tell me what you thought about Jeff Trask?" I asked.

"She brought him around occasionally," Mr. Warren said. "He was always quiet and well-mannered. He always brought Susan home at least fifteen minutes before her curfew. We're glad you're helping him. He couldn't have murdered her."

"He was good to her," Mrs. Warren said. "He isn't of our faith, yet he went to church with us once in a while. Susan hoped he would go more often." He hadn't mentioned churchgoing. Maybe this was true love.

"She'd emerged from her shell these past few months, but that was a welcome change," Mr. Warren said. "She was always an introverted girl. She even talked about attending the summer religion camp we help sponsor every year. Jeff said he might go along. We told the police we couldn't believe he killed her. He was so mild-mannered and polite."

Mrs. Warren dabbed at her eyes with a tissue she clutched in her hand. Her husband put his hand on her arm. "God will give us strength," he assured her.

They could give us no information as to Susan's activities that final Sunday. She'd left with Jeff at noon. They hadn't known anything until the police arrived at the door. As to who could have killed their daughter, they had no idea. It was after four by the time we left.

"I don't think they had a realistic view of their daughter's life," I said.

"What parent does?" Scott asked. "My parents could have figured out anytime in thirty-seven years about my sexual orientation. They never did. They didn't want to. If the Warrens are strongly religious, maybe that's what they did see."

"Or maybe that's what Susan wanted them to see."

"What we don't have is a reason for someone to kill her," Scott said.

"Yeah. So far this drug thing is a bust."

"Not funny," he said, then suggested, "Maybe Becky killed her in a fit of revenge."

To that, I had no answer. As far as I could see, Becky had no reason to kill Susan.

We stopped at the Trask home. I wanted to check on how Eric was and see whether he could tell us anything about the attack.

Eric met us at the door. His mom was out Christmas shopping. "You look okay. How're you feeling?" I said as we stepped into the living room.

White bandages covered his fingers. He reported that the doctor said he'd be fine. He wouldn't lose any body parts. "I was lucky. You saved my life."

We talked doctors for a while, then I said, "You know Roger's dead."

"Yeah, man, that's awful. Roger was cool."

"Had you talked to him since you were attacked?"

"The guys came over as a group last night. They snuck some beer past my mom. We had a great party. I'm still not up and around as much as I want, so it was great to see them."

"How'd Roger seem?"

"Normal. He told about a million jokes, like he always does."

"Who in the group was connected with Becky in selling stuff? I'm especially interested in Susan and Roger."

"Nah. Forget those two. They were pretty straight. Susan hardly ever said boo. Roger was the life of everything. He drank a little beer like everybody, but that's all. Kids hoped Roger'd be in class with them because they knew he'd keep it interesting. Everybody liked Roger."

"Everybody but one," Scott said.

"Well, yeah," Eric said.

"About drugs and the group," I reminded him.

"Well, we all bought small amounts once in a while. Most of us didn't really buy all that much. What little I know of the actual setup is that she had kid distributors at each grade level. They'd pick up stuff at her house mostly, I think, although I've never seen it. Like on Sundays, people knew to come over to the Conlans' to buy drugs."

"All people knew?"

"Well, some anyway. Maybe ten or so kids would show up."

"Who were the dealers?"

"I don't know. Some kids came over because they were friends of friends and they'd heard it was a place to buy. Some were dealers. I don't know which were which. I never asked. I was never part of it. I didn't even know their names."

"What happened Wednesday?" I asked.

He shook his head. "I don't know. Last thing I remember is the wall outside the gym doors. I didn't hear or see anything. Somebody grabbed me and then I got belted in the head. That's all until I woke up in the hospital."

"Are you covering for somebody right now?" Scott asked.

"No, Mr. Carpenter, honest," Eric replied.

In the car, I announced, "We're going to see Mrs. Twitchell."

"You've lost your mind," Scott counterannounced.

"Somebody's dealing bullshit. I intend to find out who."

"She's head of the board. They could fire you."

"She's covering up something."

"So you say. Why not check with Frank Murphy?"

"Frank is conducting a sociological tea for the good citizens of River's Edge. And I'm pissed at the idiot parents. We're going to find the murderer."

"Your job could be on the line," Scott said.

"I can handle it."

Mrs. Twitchell answered the door. She let us in but stopped us three feet inside the door.

"This is incredibly impudent and shows extremely poor judgment on your part," she said.

I barely avoided shielding my eyes from her outfit: solid white pants, clinging to the bulges around her hips and thighs, and a clinging orange-gray sweater vest that revealed amazing amounts of breast. Her red high heels gave the outfit a vague Christmas sheen.

I said, "Perhaps it is a rotten decision. If so, then I need to get what I came for."

"You have thirty seconds to explain before I throw you out. I would use that time to convince me not to have you fired in the morning."

"Bully somebody else. Becky's done something and you're covering for her like mad . . . more than usual is my guess. Why? Did she kill Susan?"

"Get the hell out of my house." Her eyes glittered angry daggers. She grabbed several folds of my overcoat and pushed toward the door. A foot taller than she, I moved less than an inch. She yelped in frustration and backed off.

"You must have had some inkling of your daughter's problems after all the reports you got at home. Don't you realize how much help your daughter needs?"

She advanced upon me again. I suspected an invitation to dinner was not forthcoming. We left with her icy silence forming glaciers behind us.

In the early-evening darkness, we drove to the White Hen on 191st and Wolf Road. Most mornings in the summer, I walk the two miles there for the daily papers. The people who work at the Mokena store are great. They make the best sandwiches. Try the chicken salad on rye, with lettuce, tomato, mustard, mayonnaise, and American cheese. Throw in a pickle from the vat on the counter and it's perfect.

We hurried to my place to eat. Scott had a speaking engagement that night.

At my place, car tracks led up the fifty-foot drive. They weren't ours. We hadn't been home. Two pairs of footsteps from the driver's and passenger's side led from the car around the house. The outside lights weren't bright enough to reveal many clues. The alarm system hadn't been tripped. It could have been cops, or those who'd been following us, or maybe itinerant Bible salesmen, or perhaps someone totally innocent.

We examined the footsteps as best we could.

"Large work boots?" Scott said.

"Sherlock Holmes read volumes from things like this," I said.

"Was he freezing his ass off in forty-five-below wind chill?" Scott's teeth chattered.

Moments later, we devoured sandwiches and beer at the kitchen table.

Scott dressed in his charcoal gray suit for the speech. He looks incredibly sexy in so many different ways. Sometimes it's when he's totally naked, other times when he's in white jockey shorts and white gym socks, or sometimes in his baseball uniform, or his tight jeans and muscle T-shirt, or a business suit —or when I see him fully dressed in front of a crowd and know I've made love to the beautiful body and person underneath. I enjoy starting lovemaking fully clothed. There's something about unzipping a man's pants, a sense of power and permission that you don't have unless intimately given or violently taken, that makes it especially sexy. Maybe it's just him, and that I love him so very much.

Before Scott left, I called Kurt Campbell. We'd talked about my stopping by earlier in the week, and after a final check with his wife, Beth, Kurt said it'd be a perfect night to pick up more packets for the union-negotiations team's meeting and for a visit. I wanted to go over information with him about the kids and teachers involved. Even with the alarm system, we didn't want to take chances with one of us alone in the house. Kurt invited us both over, but Scott was late, so he dropped me off without going in. He could visit when he came by to pick me up. In the car, I kissed him hard.

"Be careful," I warned as I got out. I'd offered to ride with him to the Harvey Holiday Inn, but he'd said not to worry. It was expressway all the way, and he'd be in a crowd.

Kurt and Beth lived in an all-brick two-story home off 143rd Street in Orland Park. They greeted me at the door. It was just past seven-thirty. We sat in front of a glassed-in fireplace. We propped ourselves up with cushions against the couch. Over the years, I'd become almost as close a friend to Beth as I was to Kurt. I explained what we'd been up to.

Beth said, "I've met George and Pete's wives at faculty parties, but I've never felt I had much in common with them. They hang around together. They're harmless enough, I've always thought, but you might want to talk to them." Beth was a thin, plain woman whose warm good humor I'd enjoyed from the first time I'd met her. While we talked, the noise from their kids drifted up from a family room. Unable to have kids of their own, they'd adopted five, who now ranged in age from six months to seven years old. Occasionally, pairs of eyes peeked around corners, followed by silly giggles. A toddler or two would drift in, bury his or her head shyly in a parental lap, and then retreat to the playroom. In the middle of the conversation, Kurt brought the baby down for a bottle, after which the child slept peacefully on his chest.

"I've know those guys for years," Kurt said. "I've found them a total pain in the ass. As athletic director, I work with them pretty closely. They push themselves hard as coaches, sometimes to little effect."

"Why keep them on?"

"Politics, length of service to the district, inertia. It would be a tremendous pain to get rid of them, and it might not work. They have factions that support them strongly."

Certain power centers exist in every school district. These seldom correspond to who is nominally in charge. In some districts, it's the athletic boosters, in others, a cabal of teachers who've taught there since the year one. I knew one district where a new math teacher came in and criticized the band program. The man was out of a job before January. Of course, there are also the old standby power centers of the janitors and secretaries. A new teacher crosses either of these at his peril, an old teacher with great discretion. I knew one teacher, new to the district—back in the days when the custodians handed out all supplies—who needed chalk. She asked for some and got two pieces. She explained that this wasn't adequate. She got two more. In frustration, after weeks of this, she went and bought her own supply. The janitor never forgave her. Fortunately, he quit within the same year.

Beth said, "Don't waste time talking about that sports crap, get to the good stuff. They both cheat on their wives."

"We only have conjecture, no real proof," Kurt said.

"Stop being so damn rational and fair," Beth said with a smile.

"That's what makes him a good union president," I said.

Beth sniffed. "It's fairly well documented by those of us in the gossip grapevine that those two fuck anything in a skirt. They go on these long hunting trips and catch far more than a few dead birds."

"Beyond cheap gossip," Kurt said, "there's the incessant bitching and moaning they do about every little thing. The inability to accept responsibility for themselves, their inability to think before they speak. They both have to take stupid pills in the morning. Nobody could be that dumb all by themselves."

"Personally," Beth said, "from the few times I've been around those two, I presume their stupidity is a congenital defect."

"The odd thing," Kurt said, "is George is good with kids. The boys on the teams respond to him, and I've heard the girls in class do, too. He understands teenagers and their problems. Now, Pete is incredibly intense. He has to win at everything. I've played poker with him. He slams the cards on the table if he loses even a small pot. He's the same at sports, even pickup games among the coaches at school. He'd knock you over if you got in his way."

"I'm not sure I could say what makes them tick," I said. "I may have saved their asses from the administration, but they'll never make sense to me."

Kurt talked about the attitude of the two coaches. As athletic director, he wanted the kids to learn fundamental skills, understand teamwork and sportsmanship, and have a little fun. Montini and Windham had the mania that so many high school coaches had. When they looked out on the field, they saw NFL football or NCAA basketball, not kids. Kurt found, and I agreed, that the tremendous pressure this put on kids at an age and with a set of emotions most of them couldn't handle was unconscionable on the part of adults.

Then again, I was strange. In high school, I wanted it to be fun, a game. I was also too much of a smart mouth. I sat out football my junior year because of my "bad attitude." In college, it was worse. They ran it like a big business. Bullshit. So I lost my student deferment and wound up in the Marines in Vietnam.

Kurt said, "You've seen those two at the games. They scream and bellow at the kids from tip-off to final buzzer. Montini's coached the team out of several wins this year. He pressures the kids into paralysis.

"But like I said, they're good with kids. I've heard they've helped a couple out in tough spots. Of course, there's some who hate them. Remember the time Montini turned the kid in for drinking?"

I nodded. Grover Cleveland had a strict policy. Any athlete caught drinking alcohol or doing drugs got thrown off the team—no questions, no appeal. The incident to which Kurt referred was when a kid had drunk a beer in his parents' house with their permission and with them present. Somebody told Montini. He reported it to the administration. They threw the kid off the team the next day. This could easily be the center of Paul's fears.

Scott bustled in around ten, stomping snow from his shoes. We heard whispering from the top of the stairs. Little voices that should have been asleep noted that Uncle Scott was here. Immediately thereafter, a little girl, maybe all of three, materialized at Scott's elbow. Within five minutes, Scott sat on the floor amid a mountain of toys, with children laughing, squealing, and climbing all over him. He's a natural with kids. Then again, he doesn't have to live with them twenty-four hours a day.

I can't stand little kids. I know that might sound odd from a teacher, but if they're under five, I am klutz personified. Plus, I've always resented the mothers who thrust their couple-month-old creature at you, as if holding them was a test.

Minutes later, Scott sprawled in a corduroy overstuffed easy chair with the two-year-old's head resting on his shoulder. In two minutes, her eyes began to droop shut. The three-year-old rested her head against Scott's side, snuggled between him and the chair arm.

Beth shook her head. "You have that effect on them every time you're here."

Scott plucked a small red fire truck from the floor and handed it to the three-year-old. The kid drove around Scott's kneecap contentedly.

"How'd you learn to do that?" Kurt asked.

"With my sister's kids when they were little," Scott replied.

It was late, but youthful demands resulted in Uncle Scott giving readings from several favorite stories before we could leave.

As we got our coats, I asked Scott whether he'd seen anybody following him. He'd checked carefully—nothing.

We hurried into the brutal cold. "Guy on the radio on my

way back said the weather's supposed to break this weekend," Scott said as we walked to the car. We were in the street. Behind us, the lights in Kurt's house went out.

Car doors slammed. I glanced down the street. Five guys ran toward us. Too late for a dash to the car or back to the house.

9

Only two attacked me and I held them off fairly easily. In the bulk of winter clothes, it was hard to get or receive a clear hit. The two of them and I grappled in the middle of the street. I glanced for a second or two where three of them surrounded Scott. A knife gleamed in the hand of the one nearest to him. I called out a warning to watch the knife. I'd been distracted too long, however. My attackers moved in, each now with his own knife out.

For several minutes, I concentrated on defending myself. I breathed deeply while they circled warily. I'd thrown my coat off to get better leverage. I shot another look at the other group.

I saw Scott fall and one of them raise his knife. I went berserk. Every fiber of jungle training to hurt, maim, kill, and destroy awoke in me beyond unreasoning fury. The insatiable rage, the freedom of blind insanity unleashed to crush a human being hurled me to rescue my fallen lover. I heard bones breaking as I freed Scott from their grasp. They backed and dragged away as I quickly checked Scott. He was alive but bleeding and unconscious.

They stumbled to their car. It started with a roar, but it spun and stuck in the snow and ice. I ran toward them and tried to pry a door open. There'd be no escape and no mercy if I got hold of them. Two of the shits lay heaped on the backseat. A third, also in the back, and a fourth from the front passenger side screamed at the driver to make the car go. With my first blow, I shattered the windshield. Through my glove, I felt the numbness beyond pain spread up my arm. The second blow with my other hand scattered the glass. I could see and hear them clearly now. I tried to grab the driver or the steering wheel.

Then the tires finally caught. The car spurted away, yanking my arm with hideous pain. My arms and left shoulder felt dead, but I hurried to Scott. He lay unconscious and losing blood. I rushed to the house. Kurt answered, saw me, and yelled to Beth to call the police. He grabbed his coat and followed me out. I was beyond caring about the cold or any pain. They and whoever sent them would pay for how badly my lover was hurt. They would feel it ten times for every ache, bruise, and cut. If he died, I would hunt them down and kill them.

By the time the police and the ambulance showed up, we'd gotten Scott inside. His breathing seemed okay and the bleeding had slowed, but nothing we did brought him around. I accompanied him in the ambulance. Kurt drove his car, and Beth followed in mine.

The emergency-room personnel buzzed around Scott, his celebrity status ensuring instant and more than adequate attention. We waited less than half an hour. Kurt and Beth accompanied me to Scott's room. The doctor told us that with the exception of a mild concussion and broken left arm, he was fine. Fortunately, he pitched right-handed. They wanted to keep him overnight for observation. When the doctor left the room, it was after two. Scott slept.

Beth said, "There's nothing more for you to do. If you're afraid to go home, come with us. We'll put you up." Kurt echoed her sentiments.

"I want to sit with him for a while," I said.

They repeated their offer, then left.

The night sounds of the hospital crept into the room. Soft-soled shoes padded by. A murmured conversation rose and faded. I placed my overcoat on the empty bed next to Scott's. I smelled clean hospital sheets. I sat next to him and took his right hand in both of mine. I watched his chest rise and fall peacefully. The new white plaster of his cast shone dully. I saw anew the freckles under his chin. I reached over and smoothed his mussed blond hair into familiar patterns. An ugly scrape stretched across his forehead. The doctor said there would be no scar. I observed carefully the outline of his legs, the mound of his genitals, the flat stomach and powerful chest and shoulders, all his six-foot-four muscle and strength at total rest. I had a horrible vision of life without him. With my fingertips, I caressed his forehead, stroked his eyebrows, nose, lips, cheeks, felt the tender skin, all that the vast crowds could see every fifth day in the summer, every bit that I saw each night. "I love you," I told his sleeping form.

He stirred momentarily, then resumed his rest. I stayed next to him a long time. The nurse came in on her rounds at one point. She smiled uncertainly and left us.

Eventually, I moved to the chair. Next thing I knew, I was awake. Winter dawn peeked around the curtains into the room. Scott slept on. I found the hospital cafeteria for some breakfast. When I got back, reporters hovered in the corridors by the nurses station. In the room, Scott lay awake, charming the nurse.

He greeted me breezily. The nurse looked disapproving. I wanted to see Windham and Montini for a direct and brutal confrontation. I presumed, while they hadn't been present the night before, that they were behind the attack. They were the adults most threatened. I couldn't see Becky as head of some vast drug conspiracy with power to order attacks. I explained this to Scott. He told me to go ahead. He'd wait for the doctor's approval to let him go. I said I'd be back to pick him up. I hadn't the slightest worry about being attacked. Tired and sore as I was, maybe a massed attack of jungle snipers might be able to slow me down. I doubted it.

First, I drove to the Montinis'. They lived in the old part of

Tinley Park, just off Oak Park Avenue and 173rd Street. I'd spent hours there last year with Pete when he'd been in trouble with the administration for the twin infractions of telling a kid to fuck off and then belting him up-side the head. The kid certainly deserved it, but Pete was stupid enough to do it in front of a whole class of witnesses. Trying to convince someone that he is an asshole when he thinks he is nobly fighting the war against recalcitrant kids and weak-willed administrators is tough, especially when you're like me and trying to do it diplomatically.

Pete wasn't home. His wife, Maria, invited me in. Pete had gone out earlier with George to the hardware store and then supposedly to George's house to fix shower tiles in the basement bath. Then they were going to watch basketball and football games all afternoon.

I liked Maria. Every time I'd been to the house, she'd stayed and quickly caught on to what I kept trying to convince Pete to do. She'd always been cheerful, offering to help in any way. Underneath her cheery exterior, she struck me as lonely and forlorn—someone who needed a friend to whom to talk. I think she was grateful to me for helping save Pete's job.

She asked me whether I wanted a cup of coffee. In her kitchen, I explained about trying to help Jeff.

"I doubt if Pete knows anything," she said. "I can't picture him being the least help in an investigation." She laughed. "Once in a while, he tries to lurk around here furtively, but he's so transparent. Men think they're so clever. He's been on the phone with George all week. He thinks I haven't noticed. Those two are up to something."

"Do they cook things up often?" I asked.

"Usually when they want to go on one of their weekend hunting trips. Sarah, George's wife, and I laugh about them. The men don't know how obvious they are. Every four months, they begin plotting and scheming. I shouldn't tell you this, but we have it planned too, so we can extort the most out of them when they ask permission. Actually, it's an enormous relief to get them out of the house. This trip is a little odd in that they just got back two weeks ago from their latest. They might be trying for a fifth one this year. They tried last year, but we put our feet down."

She explained that they usually went to several places in Minnesota. While pouring coffee, she told me that Pete didn't realize that being a teacher and having a family, he'd need to work so many extra jobs. She rarely saw him. She said, "I shouldn't tell you my problems, but those two! And George is the one that pushes them. I'd never say this in front of Sarah, but that man has to be cheating on her. He's come on to me a number of times. I slapped him hard once. Since then, he hasn't dared touch me."

I didn't blame her for not telling Sarah. The woman had six kids. She didn't need more worries.

"I don't trust him," Maria went on. "Sometimes when he looks at me, he gives me the creeps. I bet he keeps a girlfriend on the side, and that takes money, too. How any woman could want him is beyond me. He may be young and slightly handsome, but he is slime."

I thought that for some people, young and slightly handsome is enough to justify a few moments of warmth.

I decided to give George's place a try, although I suspected it would be futile.

The Windhams lived just west of Tinley in one of the new subdivisions off Eightieth Avenue. They'd bought the house before it was built. Brick covered the bottom half of the house, fake wood the top. A seven-year-old asked who I was, disappeared a moment, them came back and let me in. As I crossed the threshold, squalling and bedlam hit me stronger than the northern gusts that had buffeted us all week. Sarah's voice called from upstairs that she'd be right down. The seven-year-old with silent dark eyes led me solemnly to the living room. He pointed to a couch. I made my way through ankle-deep toys and sat down. The kid marched off.

When Sarah finally joined me, she said, "It seems like we've got five seconds of quiet, what can I do for you?"

Sarah had worked as a secretary for a few months in the English department at school. It was five years ago, just after they'd moved to town. Bright and friendly, she'd filled the part-time job to perfection. Then she'd had a run of kids and stayed home with them. I never understood why she sacrificed her degree in chemical engineering for a creep like George. Sarah was a rapidly aging twenty-eight years old. She had brown hair cut straight to her stooped shoulders, and a figure that told of too many kids too soon. Her home showed the chaos of six multiplied by the neglect of one of the parental team.

I'd seen her a few times at faculty parties since she'd quit.

I explained about helping Jeff; that I'd talked to George once; and that I wanted to ask a couple more things.

"I don't think he knew Susan," she said. "We talked about it. He said he never had her in class."

"I'm interested in all the kids, not just Susan. He'd know some of them from class or from being assistant football coach."

"Oh. I see. Well, he's running errands, then he's going to Pete's. Those two are always busy plotting some silly scheme. I wish George spent a quarter of the time helping me and the kids as he does on those stupid dreams the two of them make up. He has no idea what I go through. And he's always got a place to go." A child yelped and another bellowed. She rushed off. I heard a small smack, angry reproaches, the classic defense of "I didn't do nothing," and finally peace.

She came back and sat down heavily. She said, "Some days I'd kill for a real live adult conversation for ten uninterrupted minutes."

"Sounds like you need a good solid vacation," I said.

"I need a full-time maid, but I'd settle for a part-time husband."

At work, Sarah had never struck me as happy or sad, only frustrated and tired. "Is he always taking off?" I asked.

"He's gone whenever I need him most." She explained that their oldest boy, Steve, had broken his collarbone last spring. She had to take him to the hospital and couldn't leave the other kids. She didn't want to pay an extra ambulance fee. Her mother was out. She finally found a neighbor to watch two of the kids. . She wound up trailing three kids into the emergency room. Worse than some goddamn mother duck. George had been at a cabin in Minnesota.

Another husband escaping from the rigors of responsibility.

Sarah continued, "Those guys think they're so clever. I suppose it's safe to tell you, although you may have guessed. Pete uses these little excursions to get some on the side. He especially likes young waitresses in truck stops." She laughed. "I know George doesn't cheat. He knows I'd cut off his balls if I ever caught him. But I blame Pete for how George is. When we first married, George was so attentive and kind. He played with the kids. Always helped with the housework. But we needed money and he took the assistant coaching position. He and Pete became friends. It's been worse since then."

I asked how she found out about Pete cheating. She told me that the spring before, she'd called the cabin about Steve's arm. She got some drunk girl on the phone who sounded maybe twenty. The girl thought Sarah was somebody from the local truck stop. Before the girl caught on, she'd told Sarah how great Pete was in bed. Sarah received extensive knowledge of Pete's proclivities and tendencies.

She giggled. "I admit I didn't stop her. I suppose I could mention it to Maria, but I'm not going to be the one to tell somebody her husband's cheating. I'm not that crazy."

"George says you keep him on a pretty tight leash," I said.

She laughed. "He exaggerates. He's been doing what he wants for years. I can't even remember all of his jobs. He keeps the money coming in. Although, like everybody else, it's never enough."

By the time I got back to the hospital to pick up Scott, it was only nine-thirty.

Scott's arm hurt, but they'd given him pain pills. His comment on the wives' revelations ran along the lines of the scandalously high hetero divorce rates and their incapacity for commitment in a real relationship.

We arrived at my place before ten. I made him comfortable on the couch in front of the fireplace. Because of Scott's fame the attack had made all the newscasts. My mom called to see whether he was all right. Several of his teammates including Doug called. Not a word from his family. He didn't say anything, but I suspected it bothered him. After a half hour of phone calls, he leaned back on the couch and shut his eyes. "I'm pretty tired. Let's put the answering machine on and forget the world."

I did as he asked. Then I closed all the curtains and turned off all the lights to let the room rest in the glow from the fireplace. I put an old Peter, Paul, and Mary disc on the CD player. I sat on the couch by his chest and undressed him slowly, massaging each set of muscles as I went.

With his eyes closed, Scott muttered, "You've been threatened, and we've been attacked. We're no closer to solving the murder than we were Monday." He droned a list of negatives for nearly five minutes.

I unbuttoned his pants, slipped them over his hips, rubbed the stomach muscles. "We could stop."

"No. I want to go on. It's just ..." He shut his eyes and I continued my ministrations in silence. Peter, Paul, and Mary sang "Stewball."

"Last night, I was scared of losing you," I said.

He opened his eyes. I lost myself in their depths as I had so many times before.

"Thanks for saving me," he said. Then his voice reached its lowest thrum as he said, "I don't ever want to lose you. Not solving this murder, nothing ever is more important to me than us."

I moved up and kissed him tenderly and held him fiercely. He returned the embrace awkwardly with one arm. We stayed that way long moments. Then I returned to relaxing his muscles. The hair on his chest and legs makes the most wonderful soft blond down. We listened to an old Joni Mitchell album for half an hour while I worked on him.

Finally, he stretched his muscles, then eased back contentedly. "That feels so great," he said. I glanced at the front of his shorts. "I can see you're enjoying it." His famous right arm reached for me. Avoiding the cast on his arm proved easy. An hour later, I said I could call Meg and cancel our luncheon date. He wouldn't hear of it. He took another pain pill and we left.

Meg's place was warmth, caring, kindness, and safety. We lingered over wine and coffee, discussing life, the world, and murder. Outside of my times with Scott, I feel most comfortable at Meg's.

The temperature inched toward thirty degrees above as we drove up LaGrange Road from Meg's home in Frankfort. The first fat flakes of the next storm drifted earthward. The weather forecaster said blizzard warnings were out for northern Illinois.

The lack of cars in my driveway didn't prepare us for the two burly men standing in my living room. One I recognized as the giant from the farmhouse. The guns they showed were argument enough for us to cooperate. No kids this time—these were adults, tight-lipped and threatening. Perhaps as many as ten words were spoken, maybe as few as five, as one held his gun on us while the other handcuffed, blindfolded, and bundled us out of the house.

They led us from the front room out the back door. No possible way we could be seen by passing motorists. In the cold outside, we waited a moment. I heard the garage doors opening, car doors clicking, and a motor purring to life. They shoved us into a space that felt wider than a normal car backseat. I guessed maybe a curtained van.

"Scott?" I murmured.

"Yeah?" His voice came from inches away.

A belt up-side the head hurt like hell and convinced me that while silence at this time might or might not be golden, it would certainly be less painful. I can find violence convincing, especially when they have the guns.

By the sway of the car, I could tell we had turned right onto Wolf Road. Another right at the stop sign at 183rd Street and a steady drive. Finally, a last right followed moments later by the steady woosh onto I-80. Time felt funny under the blindfold. We had to be heading west. I presumed to the farm.

I concentrated on what I could sense: strong leather smell from the seats, stale cigar smoke, perhaps oil on gun metal. No sound of radio music or noise. I could feel the handcuffs where they clamped my wrists. They'd wedged Scott next to me on my right. That's where his reply had come from, and I would need to be more than blindfolded and then away from him for a long time to mistake his touch and smell. Our knees and legs stayed together. I moved my left leg tentatively. I got a sharp rap on the kneecap with what I guessed was a gun barrel for my efforts. No need for threats or silly nonsense, just deadly seriousness.

Finally, there was a slowing and a brief halt, as if for a stop sign; then another stretch of driving less than the first but seemingly interminable. Then came a slowing and turning, followed by the rumble of tires over gravel. The car stopped. They turned the engine off. Car doors slammed. I stirred. "Sit," a raspy voice commanded. I sat.

They spoke in murmurs. Everything seemed calm and sedate.

No one hurried. All movements seemed deliberate and at ease. They escorted us almost gently out of the car.

My feet stumbled on gravel, then crunched on packed snow. "Step down," my guide commanded. There was a space in front of my left foot, but I found the step and inched forward. It was a narrow way down, smelling of damp and mold. I counted steps taken, ten down. We walked forward. I presumed I'd be dead in a few minutes. I tried to plan a last desperate fight. Being blindfolded and handcuffed were strong arguments against such absurdity.

At last, they removed the restraints. Light flooded my eyes. I shut and covered them. They took our coats, hats, and gloves, and tied us to chairs, our hands behind our backs. A few futile questions escaped my lips, but they didn't deign to answer or even to look at us as they left.

Scott and I faced each other. As my eyes got used to the light, I realized it was only one quite weak bulb in the ceiling. They'd tied us to plastic-covered kitchen chairs in a narrow room with rough-hewn walls and a dirt floor, perhaps an old root cellar slightly expanded. A two-foot-long, two-foot-high wooden bench made up the room's only other furniture. We took inventory of each other.

Scott'd yelped when they'd yanked his arm around to tie him. In response to my questions, he claimed it didn't hurt. Then he asked, "Did Sherlock Holmes ever get caught and tied up?"

I thought, "In the movies maybe, but definitely not in the original stories."

"Right. Whatever. My question is, What are we doing wrong? Or what was he doing right? And can we do it his way next time?"

"We do seem to be up shit creek without the proverbial paddle."

"Old buddy, we don't even have a canoe," he said.

I'd managed a glance at my watch before being stuck in the chair. It was after two.

We struggled with our bonds. "I think I can move a little," Scott began.

The door burst open and Becky Twitchell made her entrance. I introduced Scott. He did not puke all over her.

Becky's blond hair cascaded down the back of her silver-fox fur. She flounced and twirled around the room. She stopped in front of me and laughed. "You stupid shit. As a school-teacher, you suck. As a detective, you haven't got a brain in your head."

She stood between Scott and me, and I couldn't see him, but suddenly Becky pitched forward. She knocked against me, then fell, slumped to the ground. She was up in an instant. Scott had caught her by surprise by raising himself and the chair enough to bang into her from behind. He'd fallen over with the effort and couldn't right himself.

"You're going to pay for that, you shit!" she said. She kicked him in the nuts, then stepped on his cast. He howled in pain. I struggled to free myself. I managed to move my chair all of two inches.

She whirled back on me and snarled, "Don't even think about it, Mason! You're history."

I looked at Scott. His gasps had turned to shallow breathing. He couldn't rise without help. Becky did not offer. In the ensuing silence, I watched in agony as Scott's grimaces of pain came further and further apart. He managed a look and a nod at me. "I'll be okay," he uttered through gritted teeth.

"Hah!" Becky said.

I looked at her in fascination. Pretty; some would say beau-tiful. She might turn heads on the street—people wondering, Isn't that the young actress? No amount of makeup skillfully and beautifully applied could hide her cold eyes, hard-set lips, and iron-set jaw.

"Since we're going to be dead, could you satisfy my curios-ity?" I said.

She leaned against the door. I hoped her arrogance would

lead her to give us information. What earthly good it could do for two very captured victims, I had no idea, but I wanted to know.

"You've got a hell of a nerve," she said.

"If I'm going to be dead, what difference does it make?" I saw that Scott breathed normally. I caught his eye. He sighed.

Becky noticed the look. "You know, you guys should be pleased I'm not prejudiced against gay people. My uncle's one of you. So I just hate you on general principles, not from stereotypical narrow-mindedness."

"How nice," I said. "We'll nominate you for the Nobel Peace Prize." It took her only a few seconds to cross the room and slap my face hard. I tasted blood.

She paced the room. I let a few minutes pass before I asked, "Why is Susan dead?"

She stopped and looked at me. "I don't know. She should be alive."

"She wasn't a victim of your revenge?"

"She never crossed me." She sighed. "Susan had grown up a lot lately. I take credit for that. Still a little too religious for my taste. But lately, she'd learned the way the world really works."

"How's that?" I asked.

"Get yours first," Becky replied. "Susan was more thickheaded than most. It took her longer to catch on."

"What happened the night of the party?"

"Jeff and Susan left. People came and bought drugs. Then I went home."

"Who would want to kill her?"

For the first time, Becky paused thoughtfully before speaking. "I've considered it from a lot of angles. I can't see anyone doing it. Susan was nice. Quiet, but people were beginning to warm up to her before she got it."

"Why is Roger dead?"

"Well." She took a deep breath. "That is a whole other problem. That was your fault."

"Could you help Scott up before you tell us the error of our ways?"

When she hesitated, I added, "Come on, Becky. We're going to die. At least let us be comfortable."

It was a struggle but she righted him. Dirt stuck in his hair and smeared the right side of his face. She pulled the ropes tighter around him but then stayed clear of both of us as she talked.

"Poor Roger," she began. "He really was a stupid jock. If men or boys had brains, they wouldn't fuck up so much."

"How did Roger fuck up?"

"He planned to run to you and tell you the truth. The right people caught him before he could get to you."

"What did he know?"

"Everything. He'd been one of my dealers for years. It doesn't do for fringe players to know too much and want to tell. He followed me to a meeting. We presumed you sent him, although he denied it."

"We didn't send him."

"Who cares? He stole records and everything from the farmhouse. They caught him with them. He died swiftly and relatively painlessly, which I hope I won't be able to say about you guys."

She did another flounce and twirl around the room. She landed in front of me. "Even if you escaped, fellas, you wouldn't get far. The temperature's on its way down, the wind is up, and good old John Coleman on Channel Five has predicted a blizzard. Hell of a winter. Too bad you'll miss the rest of it." She laughed.

"Why attack Eric?"

This time I got a derisive snort out of her. "You thought he was such a buddy. Actually, Eric was the ultimate go-between. His problem was that he went to talk to you before getting permission. I've been suspicious of the son of a bitch for a long time now. He and I had a big fight Monday after school. He'd been trying to horn in on my territory. I wanted to put him out of business. I followed him to your classroom on Wednesday and listened outside the door. I heard his lies and how he tried to screw me. That pissed me off. I got hold of a few of my staffers, and we gave him a lesson. He's learned to behave."

"He knew who attacked him?" I asked.

"Of course."

"I don't believe you about Eric," I said. "He knew me. We were friends."

I got laughed at for that piece of fatuousness.

"How does Paul fit in all this?" Scott asked.

"He's convenient, hunky, popular, safe, and comfortable. He's also good in bed. He can fuck forever. And he deals drugs."

I shook my head. "One thing I don't get is that if Susan wasn't killed because of drugs, why'd she die?"

"Ask Jeff. Maybe he was jealous."

"Of what?"

Becky said, "Susan fucked all kinds of guys. She'd learned to have fun. That drip Jeff was well on his way out of the picture. He could be Mr. Nerd. All those guys are such fucking wimps. They never want to take chances. That's why they put me in charge of the drugs at school."

"Who put you in charge?" I asked.

"I did." We turned and saw George Windham, handsome and smiling, standing in the doorway.

"You!" I said.

He sat on the old log bench and leaned back against the wall. His voice grated on me as he talked.

"Of course me. Do you think I can support six goddamn kids on a teacher's salary? I got tired of working five jobs. A couple years ago, I picked up with some old friends from college. I moved into the market. Eventually, they gave me the concession for Grover Cleveland. Actually I do all the local high schools now: Stagg, Andrew, Lincoln Way, Providence. In a year or two, I'll get all of Joliet."

"You're nuts," Scott said.

"You're the one who's tied up, not me," George pointed out, then continued: "Some of us aren't lucky enough to have the natural talent to be an athletic millionaire. Most of us are average working stiffs."

"They're fucking assholes," Becky said.

"You can leave, Becky." He said this quietly but with angry command very near the surface.

She slammed the door on her way out. He chuckled to himself briefly, then walked over to us, wearing a nasty smile. "We could bury you under the barn, or maybe fix up a lover's quarrel."

"You dragged Pete into this with you?"

He laughed. "No. Pete is a quite willing participant. You know those camping trips? Besides our sexual forays, they were to pick up drugs smuggled over the Canadian border. He helped deliver. He never knew I was in charge." He laughed long and hard. "I couldn't resist stringing him along. I didn't want to test his gentle suburban heart with too much truth. He's a useful, friendly nothing. He followed you, then reported to me so I could send the kids out to frighten you away. The kids weren't good enough, unfortunately. I underestimated you two. That won't happen again. Now you have to be put out of the way permanently."

"Did you kill Susan?"

"For what it's worth, I didn't. She'd begun selling, of course. Eric was breaking her in slowly."

"Becky told us about Eric, but she said Susan wasn't dealing."

"Eric's one of my top lieutenants. I didn't mind Becky attacking him. A little friendly competition among the help is good. Besides, kids need to be taught a lesson from time to time. This was Eric's. He's learned. Becky will get hers soon. As for Susan, of course she dealt."

"Were Jeff and the others on the team dealing?" I asked.

"Not the whole team. Jeff certainly. Paul, of course."

"Paul's a dealer?" I asked.

He crossed the room and patted me on the head. He put his

hand under my chin, lifted my head so that my neck strained. "You poor sap." He explained about how Paul'd been part of the organization for years, that the boy'd gotten nervous since Susan's death, afraid the whole drug operation would come out, fearful his connection to drugs would surface and, despite the protection of Pete Montini and his father's influence, school district policy would be invoked and he'd be off the team and very probably out of a career. "We used his little fears to keep him in line," George said. He gave a wintry smile. "The pressure's been a little tough for Paul the perfect, but he understands who's boss."

I remembered Paul in tears, and I could picture George or Becky as merciless tormentor.

George continued his explanation. There'd been different kids, numerous former students whom he'd recruited over the years. From their school records, he knew which kids had had drug problems while in school. After they graduated, he'd meet and talk to selected ones. Eventually, the lure of big bucks got them on board. Not one refused. Becky had gotten Paul involved. He finished, "All this won't make any difference to you. You're going to be quite dead in a very short time."

"But Becky said Jeff wasn't dealing. Jeff said he wasn't dealing."

George laughed. "You have to stop being so trusting. I know every inch of this operation. Becky's only found out in the last few days who's really in charge. She likes to act quite important and knowledgeable. I used to find that useful and amusing. Her blindness and stupidity had their uses. She's a very low-level staffer. Buying from her those couple times, while mildly risky, was part of my cover. Why would the drug kingpin buy from a kid? That shows stupidity, not a controlling genius."

"Do Paul's parents know he deals?"

"Deals and does drugs," he corrected. "They probably figured it out." As far as George knew, the Conlans at this point simply wanted to protect their precious Paul, and their standing in the community. They didn't want their kid tainted by a drug scandal. He guessed Mr. Conlan had used his position on the school board to protect his son. "You guys were the problem, not the silly parents. Every time you stirred something up and made it look like Jeff didn't kill her, you threatened all of us. Death and drugs don't mix. We couldn't risk an investigation into the group. The police get nasty in the suburbs when kids start to die."

"Do you really think you'll get away with this?" I asked.

He gave a winning smile. "You have to remember what we teach in school. Don't mess with drugs. You did. You lose. Your disappearance will be investigated. Your bodies may even be found in a year or two. Who cares? For now, the press could be fed information about how gay you are. That'll cloud the issue sufficiently."

"I had suspicions about your dumb act," I said.

"Yeah. The whole thing was a joke. Who'd believe a school-teacher was the center of the drug ring at a high school? What better cover could there be?"

I tried to think of a plea convincing enough to save our lives. Nothing.

He got up, opened the door, and gave us a pitying look. "You're alive because the damn snow has delayed everything. Be patient. You'll be dead soon enough." He left.

After several minutes' silence, I said, "I vote we confess to everything and beg for mercy."

"If that was an attempt at humor, I missed it," Scott said.

"Sorry. I'm scared."

"Me, too," he said.

My eyes scanned the room desperately for something to help us. The room contained only the chairs, rope, light, bench, and us. "Can you move around so I can see the knots?" I asked.

Laboriously, he inched himself around 180 degrees. Becky'd retied him more tightly, but he managed it. I eyed the knots. "It's doable if I get the time," I said. I began my own 180-degree turn. It took me far longer than him. I was tied much tighter, with less movement allowed for my feet and ankles. It might have been twenty minutes, surely no less.

We inched our chairs back to back. We managed to mush my fingers painfully. We lost precious minutes before the feeling began to return.

I felt the rough edges of the rope, moved my hands to the first knots. I stared at the door, willing it to stay closed. Any interruption and we wouldn't be left alone again.

Before the first knot parted, sweat made my fingers slick. The stiffness and soreness in my shoulders and arms from the night before made the task more arduous. While this eternity passed and I worked frantically, Scott said, "I have to take a piss."

"Sherlock Holmes and Watson never went to the john."

Scott said, "So they were constipated for thirty years. I gotta go."

"If this is your attempt at humor"—I breathed hard from the tension of my exertions—"I am not amused. If you're serious, I have only unpleasant alternatives to offer you."

"Hey, easy." I heard the hurt in his voice.

I paused in my work. "Sorry," I said.

"Me, too," he said.

By the time the second knot came undone, sweat dripped off the tip of my nose. Several drops got into my eyes, making them sting from the salt.

We heard movement outside the doorway. I froze for an instant, then worked more frantically. The noise passed. It sounded like somebody dragging something heavy along the passage. My mind conjured up the image of a dead body being hauled off for burial. I winced at the thought and returned to the knots. I hoped whoever'd gone past didn't decide to check in on us on their return trip.

When I'd looked, I'd seen five basic knots. The third one felt easier. The fourth knot took less than a minute. I took deep breaths to calm myself. Scott spoke a few words of comfort.

The fifth knot wouldn't budge. I tried inching to my left to get a better grip and almost tipped us over. I swore and tossed my head to get the sweat off my face.

Then I felt it give. The rest of the untying went clumsily because our muscles were numb from the almost-constant confinement. At least now we were trapped but free. I glanced at my watch. A couple minutes after three.

"Now what?" Scott murmured.

"We go out the door, back the way we came, up the stairs, to the farmhouse, grab the incriminating records that Roger had, steal a car, and drive back to Chicago in a blinding snowstorm."

"Piece of cake," he said, giving me a look.

I listened intently at the door. I heard nothing. I turned the handle. It wasn't locked. I inched it open. Darkness seeped down the stairs five feet ahead of us. I saw no one. I inched the door farther open. The light was dimmer than in our room but sufficient. I risked a look. A passage to the left with no one visible in it led off to a total blackness. A couple inches to the right, a cinder-block wall extended five feet, then squared to turn under the stairs.

I opened the door wide. Scott took a place beside me. We observed carefully. Nothing moved. We heard the hum of electricity.

"Which way?" Scott asked.

"I thought I heard Becky and George go that way." I pointed up the stairs. "That passage looks like a dead end."

I guessed the root cellar was part of a larger basement complex. Piles of half-sawn boards, along with hammers and nails scattered about, spoke of recent attempts at renovation. Silence reverberated from the opening on our left. We crept up the stairs. Two solid oak doors, both with glass panes in them, met us at the top. One led outside, the other to what looked like a tiny kitchen.

"Are we in the farmhouse?" Scott whispered.

"I don't think so. This basement is too big for a house."
Peering through the windowpane to the outside was little help,
even though it was daylight. Since we'd been captive, the storm
had struck in full fury. The wind howled and the snow blew
almost vertically, making it difficult to see. The door shook as
powerful gusts struck it. I thought I could see the vague shapes
of cars off to our left. The angle was wrong, but I thought I
detected the outline of the house off to our right.

Scott put his nose against the glass and peered to our left.
"I don't see anybody," he said. "We can come back at our leisure
for the records, say sometime in July 1998."

I nodded. I eased the door open. The wind whipped it out of
my hand. It crashed against the wall and swung wildly back.
My left shoulder took a solid thunk. I held the door firmly as
we slipped through and ran like hell. I tried to see to the right
for a glimpse of the house, but the wind swirled and whipped
stinging snow into my eyes. I turned to the left. Standing upright
was difficult at times as we fought the wind and moved toward
the car. Worse, we didn't have overcoats, hats, or gloves. In the
relatively short distance, the bitter cold ripped through our
winter clothes. Numbness spread over my face and hands.
Closer now, we could see two cars and a semi-truck. We passed
a cop car and jumped into a Range Rover with the engine still
warm and clicking. We sat in the front seat blowing on our
gloveless hands. After a couple seconds of this, we ransacked
the glove compartment, under the seats, behind the sun visor.
No keys.

"Now what?" Scott said.

"You hot-wire the car and we escape."

"I do what?"

▄ 10 ▄

I stared at him. "Don't say what I know you're going to say."

"I can't hot-wire a car."

"I told you not to say that." I glared at him. "You're supposed to be the butch macho mechanic in dirty overalls in this relationship! You told me you could fix anything."

"I can, but I can't hot-wire cars. I was a good little kid. I never did that stuff. I could put a new engine in for you."

"Not tonight." I stared out the window. I knew we wouldn't be running or walking to safety. Besides our not having winter outerwear, our tracks would make it easy for them to follow us in the snow. Even if the highways remained open, I doubted if anybody'd be on the road. If we tried it cross-country through the woods and even if they didn't follow us and if we managed to walk in a direct line to help, we'd never make it. The woods probably extended only a mile or so; but in this kind of storm, keeping aware of direction could be extremely difficult. It would be far more likely that we'd die hopelessly lost in the middle of a snow-drenched expanse of nowhere.

Between gusts of wind, I could barely make out all the buildings through the windshield. We sat twenty feet beyond the barn, on the far side of the house. The immense barn stretched behind and to the left of us. Ahead and slightly to the right was the farmhouse. Today, it blazed with light that penetrated even through the storm. A lone bulb shone from the barn.

Scott grabbed my arm. "Someone's coming." He pointed toward the house. A hunched-over figure hurried toward us through the storm. We ducked down. "Grab him if he opens the door," I whispered.

Moments passed. A car door slammed, an engine revved, and tires complained as they tried to grip their way through the drifts. The sounds of the other car moved away. We eased back up. The wind roared and nobody moved outside.

Suddenly, Scott opened his door. Snow and wind rammed into the compartment. He rushed to the other vehicles. He opened doors on each one and searched inside. He leaped back into the Range Rover and slammed the door.

"No keys," he said.

"Shit." I gave him a narrow look. Snow melted in his hair. The blue of his eyes and shadows on his face shown starkly, emphasizing his ruggedly handsome looks.

"I don't like that cop car being here," I said.

He leaned against the door, arms clutched around his chest, attempting to keep warm. "Maybe they're investigating and could save us?"

That was too much to hope for, I thought. The snow lay deep on the cop car. It'd been there for hours. They probably owned the local cops. I would, if I had an operation like this.

"We could use the cops' radio to call the state police," Scott said.

"If we're in range. Besides, where would we wait for them to rescue us? Sooner or later, they'll discover we're gone. It could take hours or days for them to rescue us in this weather. Plus, they could be in on the drug operation."

I gazed into the deepening snow. Suddenly, I grinned. "The keys are in the house, right?"

"Probably."

"So all we need to do is get inside and get the keys, right?"

"Right." He paused. "How do we do that?"

I blew on my hands. "We create a diversion."

"Right. A diversion. How?"

"We burn the barn down."

"Uh-huh. The cold has gotten to your brain."

"It's old. It's wooden. They've reinforced it, but I bet it would go easily.

"What if the guys with the keys all run to the barn with the keys in their pockets?"

"I don't know. I think my scheme is worth a try. I'm open to other suggestions."

He looked at the barn, the house, the other cars, the swirling snow, and to me. Our breath began to steam up the inside of the windows.

"Isn't the barn their factory, probably the storehouse? If we burn it, won't that ruin all the evidence?" Scott asked.

"Do you think I care about that if we can get away?"

"Maybe the guy who left will come back. We can jump him and get his keys."

"Maybe he'll never come back," I said. "We could freeze waiting for him. If we do burn it but then they catch us, we at least know we cost them a bundle."

Scott squinted out the window.

"The main door to the barn is closer than the door they took us to. We'll try that first," I said.

"What if it's locked?"

"Why should they lock up? They're the bad guys. Probably mob-connected. Nobody robs them. Besides, this is rural Illinois, home of the pristine good guys. Nobody locks up."

"Well, they should," Scott said.

We rushed to the barn door. I glanced through a filthy window set in weather-scarred wood. No lights shone here. We pushed gently at the sliding door. It wouldn't budge. "Push hard," I commanded. The door squeaked horribly, but the wind tossed the noise away. We slipped inside. The door groaned as we shut it.

"They could oil the damn thing," Scott said.

I shivered in the coolness of the barn. It'd never be a sauna, but the warmth felt fantastic after the bitter outdoors. I let my eyes adjust to the dimness. Bales of hay towered to the ceiling two stories above us. Three desks, two filing cabinets, and four swivel chairs sat off to our left in a mini-office arrangement. A path led between the bales. We followed it. The barn had to be over one hundred fifty feet long, but the bales of hay ended halfway. A solid wall, obviously of new vintage, greeted us. We inched along it until we came to a door. We peered through the glass into a workroom that must have covered a large portion of the rest of the barn. We clicked open the connecting door and inched inside. Computers sat next to piles of brown plastic envelopes.

In the middle of one table sat a gym bag. I checked inside. Mechanic's clothes along with clear plastic bags with white powder sat inside. I read Eric's name on a crumpled I.D. tag attached to the side with string. If I was inclined to doubt George and Becky, I now had visual confirmation.

No time to be pissed off about that. On the far side of the room, Scott opened a plastic bag. "This is 'black tar,'" he said.

I raised an eyebrow.

"The league in its antidrug program made us sit through these classes two hours every day for a week during spring training last year. This is 'black tar,' a high-grade form of Mexican heroin worth five thousand dollars an ounce."

I gave a low whistle. "Explain the rest later," I whispered. I glanced around.

I could see across to where the door I'd looked through minutes before led out. It was set at such an angle, however, that the rest of the room hadn't been visible to me then.

We returned to the front portion of the barn. "The hay should do nicely for a fire," I said. It almost didn't, however. Neither of us had a match.

"I feel incompetent," Scott said.

We ransacked the desk drawers. "Doesn't anybody smoke anymore?" I complained. Finally, back in the workroom, I found matches in the kitchen drawer and hurried back to the front. In the ten-foot space between bales and doors, we prepared two heaps of loose hay, one on each side of the tunnel. Because of his arm, Scott worked slower than I.

"That's enough," I said. "I wish we had a convenient can of kerosene. I guess we can't have everything. You done over there?"

He stood with the last bits of straw in his right hand, staring fixedly at where he'd been working. He pointed. I joined him. An open box sat in the middle of the bundle. I cleared away more of the hay. The word BROOMS printed in dark black letters stared back at me. We gaped at the arsenal in front of us. "Oddest damn brooms," I said. We pulled straw off three more coverings. I opened them. Warfare filled the boxes: handguns, assault rifles, machine guns. Other labels read LAMPS, PLATES, GLASSES. We tried a couple more boxes. All guns and ammunition. From one of the open boxes, I grabbed a machine gun and handed it to Scott. I seized ammunition and passed some to him. "This is going to make a large bang when it goes up," I said as I took a machine gun for myself.

"Uh, Tom," Scott said.

He held the machine gun by the barrel in one hand, the ammo in the other. He looked pale.

"Problem?"

"I've never fired a gun. Never killed anybody. You're supposed to be the fierce, dark-haired, hairy-chested butch ex-Marine of this relationship."

I took the gun and slammed ammunition into it and gave it back. I pointed to the trigger. "Press here. The bullets come out this end. Be sure to point that end at bad guys."

He gulped, nodded.

I hadn't shot a gun in nearly twenty years, but I was ready if somebody started shooting at me. I gave Scott what assurances I could.

We set up a trail of hay to give us time to get out before the fire got to the ammunition. I didn't know how long it would take to catch, but I didn't want to risk an explosion while we were near. I didn't know how many bales contained guns, and I didn't want to take any chances. We opened the main door a crack. The wind blew our fuse to hell and gone. We closed the door, tried again, attempting to keep the trail out of the wind. We had to do it three times before we gave up.

"Forget it," I said. "We'll take our chances." I walked to our starter clumps of hay. I threw lit matches on both. We opened the door. I glanced back before we heaved it shut. Fire licked at the edges of the bales. We ran to the side of the barn away from the house. We hurried along the wall to the far end. No lights shone on the side of the barn. We dashed across the last gap to the house, trusting to the storm and gathering darkness.

On the side of the house out of the wind, we halted. I peered around the edge. The cold barely penetrated through my nervous energy. I could see four vehicles lined up together. The one that'd left while we hid in the Range Rover was back, plus another. By standing carefully one to a side, we could look through an uncurtained window into a starkly barren kitchen. The six-foot-nine guy from the other night shoved Becky toward a door. She'd been tied and gagged. George and a fat woman with a bulbous nose and a Rouyn Police patch on her shoulder chatted amiably. The cop drank from a Strohs beer can and puffed on an ugly black cigar. She had her unshod feet on top of the kitchen table where George sat. The other one, who had brought us from my house, stood near the sink, coat off, revealing a cop's uniform shirt.

I pulled my head down from the window. "They've got Becky," I said.

"They can keep her," Scott said.

I stuck my nose around the corner of the house and looked back at the barn. Suddenly, I saw Pete hurrying across the open space from the barn. At first, I thought he'd discovered the fire. Looking at the aged structure, however, I could see no signs yet. He entered the house. Through the window and despite the wind, I heard angry recriminations.

Scott said, "They've discovered we're missing."

They all spilled from the house toward the side entrance to the barn. Two wore half-buttoned coats that flapped in the gale. Besides the cop, George and the giant carried guns. I hoped they weren't too soon. I examined the barn through the swirling snow. Smoke oozed from openings, to be caught by the raging wind.

George yanked open the side door. Pete began gesticulating wildly. They'd discovered the fire. They ran to the front of the barn. They seemed to abandon any thought of us. My stomach turned queasy at the thought of dying in the conflagration, forgotten by our captors.

We rushed around to the back of the house, up the porch, and through the door. We paused in a back entryway, listening.

"We have to hurry," I said. "The house and cars could all go if that thing explodes big enough."

We strained our ears for the slightest sound. Nothing. We rushed through rooms throwing open drawers, dumping contents at random. We checked surfaces, coat pockets, everywhere for keys. No luck on the first floor.

We paused at the bottom of the stairs.

"We don't want to be trapped up there," Scott said.

I looked out the windows. The five of them ran frantically in and out the side barn door. They seemed to be trying to save as many drugs as they could. If it was me, I'd be petrified of an explosion and be in a car headed out. Maybe only the few bales we opened had guns and ammo. Maybe there wouldn't be an explosion. Maybe they had a fire-protection system that could stop the fire.

"We've got to keep looking," I said. We raced upstairs. On the right were two bedrooms. The first I guessed was the old master bedroom converted to an office. Open books lay strewn over an old oak school desk. No keys on it. Coats and jackets lay thrown over a dilapidated couch. Nothing in the pockets. On the way out, I snatched a coat and threw it to Scott and grabbed one for myself. The second room had two tied and gagged figures: Paul Conlan and Becky Twitchell. We untied them. I wished there was a way to leave Becky gagged. I looked out the window. Flames licked out the roof and side of the barn in several places.

"Thanks for saving us," Paul said.

"What happened?" Scott asked.

"Later," I said. "Do either of you know where the car keys are? Especially to the Range Rover."

"Third floor," Becky said. Her hair lay in twisted and ragged strands. Red welts covered the left side of her face. Her fox fur was filthy and ripped in many places. Paul looked intact physically but a wreck emotionally.

We rushed up to the top floor. It was one huge room. Three beds with dressers next to them ran along each of the long walls. On top of one of the dressers, sets of keys sat next to wallets and change. We grabbed all that we could see.

We ran to the top of the stairs, listened carefully, then rushed down to the second floor. I hurried back into the office. I pulled up at the desk. "Becky, are these the ledgers Roger had?"

She shrugged. "I don't know."

I shoved a stack at Paul and grabbed another for myself. I

paused at the phone and yanked the cord out of the wall. "Any more of these?" I asked.

"Only one in the kitchen."

We hurried to the top of the stairs. I heard voices. "Is there another way down?" I asked the teenagers.

They shook their heads no.

The voices receded. We ran on tiptoe down the stairs. Out front, Pete, George, and the cop backed away from the barn. We turned to the rear of the house. In the kitchen, the male cop and the giant stood at the sink. The big guy whimpered in pain while the cop gazed openmouthed into the sink. The whimpering one had his arm under gushing water from the faucet. I saw bits of hideously blackened skin dangling from his arm. As we entered the kitchen, they turned to stare at us.

Scott pointed his machine gun at the ceiling and pressed the trigger. Shots roared through the kitchen. "On the floor or die," he commanded.

They dropped.

"Did I do that right?" he asked.

"You betcha!" I said.

He let off another round into the ceiling. "Kill them if they move," he ordered. I jerked the phone chord out of the wall.

We all herded out the back door. I hoped, as Scott did, that his commands would hold them for a few moments. We ran toward the cars. Behind us, I heard shouts. I glanced back. The gunfire had alerted the others that something wasn't right. George, followed by Pete and the cop, hurried in our direction.

Gunshots whistled overhead. Scott and I turned and fired rapid bursts. No one fell, but they moved more cautiously. Slogging and stumbling through the snow added to our frustration and haste. However, if it hampered us, it also slowed them. I didn't want to get trapped into a shoot-out. We were on their terrain and who knew what other firepower they might have hidden in other caches around the farm? We reached the cars.

Encumbered by the ledgers, Paul and I ran several steps behind the others. Scott swung into the driver's seat. I scrambled into the passenger side. "Can you drive with your arm?" I asked.

"Yes." His cold hands fumbled with the keys.

"The barn's going to go any second," I said.

"I'm hurrying," Scott said.

The kids sat in the back. The three closed in warily. I kept the door open, half in the car, machine gun ready to repel any charge. The first set of keys Scott tried didn't work. They come closer. Several small explosions came from the barn. He tried the second set. The car started. I leapt in and slammed the door. Scott swung the wheel and snow and stones spun from the tires as we plowed toward the driveway. The window next to me shattered. I felt glass bite into my cheek and blood ooze from the side of my face.

"You're hit," Becky screamed.

Scott swung the wheel crazily.

"I'm all right! Drive! Get us the hell out of here!"

At the end of the gravel drive five minutes later, Scott swung a fast left.

Behind us, no one followed. In front, snow swirled in the headlights. As we entered the highway, a tremendous explosion tore through the early evening. Bright flame blossomed in the sky behind us. "I hope that caught the other cars," I said.

"Or that we have all the sets of keys," Scott said. I doubted this. At least the cop would have her keys. Too bad we didn't have time to disable the other cars.

"Are you all right, Tom?" Scott asked.

I held a handkerchief to my face. They'd have to dig some glass out of my scalp, but the bullet had missed. We rigged up an old blanket from the back to keep the wind outside at bay. I told Scott I'd live.

"How far to town?" he asked.

I thought back. "A few miles this way," I said.

Becky said, "It only has three cops, but they're all bought and paid for."

"We can't risk going back. If they even get one car out, they'll be close behind. We'll have to take our chances with the cops ahead of us and hope those behind won't get a chance to use the CB in the cop car. If we make it to the interstate, we should be safe," I said.

Snowdrifts crossed the road in numerous places. In other spots, sheets of ice covered the pavement. I wanted to go a thousand miles an hour. Scott drove carefully. Only a few hardy travelers joined us on the road this early evening. A few miles later in the last grays of almost night, I saw red and blue lights rotating in the distance ahead of us.

"Shit, they must have gotten a call through," I said.

I glanced out the back window. No one followed. Paul looked pale and shaken. Becky drummed her fingers against the armrest.

The cop car sat behind a one-foot drift that crossed the road.

Scott slowed our car and shoved it into a lower gear. He aimed straight at the cop car. An arm with a gun reached out the cop car's window facing us. I tore away the blanket covering mine, extended the machine gun, and sent a spray of bullets in their direction. With steady insistence, we bore down on them. I shot as fast as I could, but with the jouncing and sliding of the Range Rover, I only managed to spray a line of bullets over their trunk. I guessed it was enough. The gun and arm disappeared. Our superior fire-power and implacable approach had its effect on the cops. They began backing and sliding away. Scott never swerved. He plowed straight through the snowdrift. Scraping the back fender of the cop car, the Range Rover rumbled and rattled over and through the snowdrift. I almost dropped the machine gun.

I looked back. The cop car spun its wheels a moment, then took off after us.

"What if they call other cops?" Scott asked.

"They won't. Calling would be to our advantage. They need us dead," I answered.

Scott sped faster.

"They're catching up," I said.

Scott nodded. "Everybody hold on." I took a last look back. Maybe thirty feet separated us. I grabbed hold of the seat and the dashboard and planted my feet on the floor. We hit a long patch of ice. Just at the far edge, Scott jammed on the brakes. We swerved. Scott released the brake, fought the wheel, turning into the skid. Left, right, the wheel spun crazily. Then I felt the tires catch. We sped on into the evening.

Out the rear window, the cop car twirled to the edge of the road, onto the shoulder, then did a graceful flip onto its roof into a drift five feet below. We sped on.

The radio carried some good news. The blizzard was to miss Chicago and blanket southeastern Wisconsin. We'd be in the backlash of wind-drifted snow, but they promised less than an inch of new precipitation. Small drifts slowed us as we raced north. We passed no one on the road in either direction. Usually, we drove around drifts, sometimes over and through them. The car was a good one, and Scott drove well. The side of my face hurt.

Now that we'd eluded the cops, I asked Paul and Becky how they'd run afoul of George and the crowd. They had done it separately, neither knowing the other was present.

Paul had driven out earlier. He'd confronted George with the killing of Roger. Becky had told Paul of the new murder only minutes before we'd seen him yesterday. That's why he'd been so upset. Paul threatened George that he would tell all. George told him he would tell no one.

Becky, meanwhile, had opened her mouth once too often. George had waited outside the room when he heard her talking to us. When he disciplined her, she tried a half-baked blackmail scheme, now that she knew he headed the drug operation. George hadn't been all that fond of Becky in general. He'd laughed at her and had her tied up and thrown in with Paul. As we drove, Paul blurted out bits and bursts of information about the drug network at school. He seemed anxious to get his version of the truth off his chest. Becky seemed to be calculating the benefits of coming clean.

We found a lone gas station at the Ottowa entrance to Interstate 80. It was open. Scott and I kept our machine guns with us. I didn't trust Becky and maybe not Paul. The cops might have been okay enough to call ahead. Who knew who was in on what? The guy on duty saw us, binged open the cash register, and started handing us money.

"We only want to use the phone," I said.

"Forget the pay phone, use mine." He handed it over the counter. I saw a soft-drink cooler, a deli for sandwiches and salads, a counter for candy bars and newspapers. Country-and-western music twanged softly in the background. The place had a comfortable warmth.

The cashier raised his eyebrows when I asked the operator for the number of the River's Edge police station. They found Frank. He said not to worry. He'd get cops we could trust out here.

The guy at the counter insisted we didn't have to pay when we ordered sandwiches. I left him a twenty on the counter. Scott finally got his chance to use the john.

An hour later, three snowplows and four police cars drove up together.

They took our weapons and our statements. Frank's preliminary talk and the name Scott Carpenter helped them get over their initial disbelief. More state police and finally sheriff's cars began to arrive. Part of the original crowd left and returned. They confirmed our stories.

The deejay on the country-western station told us it was five degrees below zero and heading down. The wind blew tiny puffs of flakes wherever it wished.

While waiting for the cops to arrive, I'd paged through the ledgers. I removed the one for River's Edge that mentioned most of the people connected with Susan's murder. I wanted to use this as leverage to get information from them. Tampering with evidence, I know, but I left them volumes enough to convict anybody they rounded up. From what I could catch in my hasty inspection, far more people than I originally imagined were involved in pushing drugs at school.

A doctor cleaned up my skin early that evening. He said I didn't need stitches, and doubted whether I'd have any scars.

As the weather cleared, the press drifted in. We made official statements to the cops. The team publicity crowd showed up.

No one had died in the explosion. George and Pete had walked off into the storm and hadn't been captured. The people at the farm had managed to use the radio in the cop car, but instead of chasing us, they went back to saving drugs, so when the explosion came, it went up in flames with the other vehicles. The state cops found the local cops and the giant huddled around the house's smouldering embers. It had caught when the barn blew.

They had taken the three to the county jail. With Becky and Paul giving evidence and with the information in the ledgers, most of the story came out.

Around seven, Carolyn Blackburn and Oliver Sandgrace showed up. Carolyn gave us smiles and congratulations. Sandgrace presented us with frowns and apologies. The two of them thanked us profusely for uncovering the whole scheme. We were heroes. How nice. I had the most incriminating ledger for River's Edge hidden, however. At eight, we got out of there.

In the back of the cop car that returned us home, I spoke softly: "We're going to the basketball game tonight."

"For what? I only want to sleep for a week."

"We need to catch a murderer tonight," I said.

We arrived at my place at 9 P.M. and at school by 9:15. First, we stopped at the gym. Lights blazed over crammed bleachers. The sophomore game was in the last quarter. The varsity game would start at 9:30. Faculty, students, and parents jammed the hallways around the gym. The heat of three thousand bodies bundled for winter emanated from this part of the school. We stood in the entrance, taking in the scene. The kids on the court, their outsized uniforms bagging over skinny bodies, called and yelled to one another. The home crowd made happy and pleased noises. Our team led by fifteen points. Scott and I turned our backs on the lights and happiness. I saw Eric and the Conlans. I'd called Jeff and his mom from the gas station. They sat near the doors. Most of those we wanted to see had arrived.

We trudged down darkened hallways and up silent stairs. The cool of winter seeped closer as we moved farther from the gym. I had the ledger tucked safely under my overcoat. A copy of the incriminating pages, freshly minted in my electronic library, had been committed to the U.S. mail as we drove to school.

Carolyn Blackburn stood in the school office. Dim emergency lights pushed long shadows into silent corners. We talked in the semidarkness. Back at the interstate, I'd asked for this meeting. Now I explained the details of what I intended to do.

"I trust you," she said. She agreed to my plan.

I handed Carolyn a list. "I need to see these people separately. Could you telephone anybody whom we haven't seen already downstairs and get them to come over, and would you call them up here one at a time in this order?"

She glanced at the list. "It's a little late but I'll get them up here. I'll make the calls first." She sat at the secretary's desk and began punching numbers on the phone. Carolyn said we could use her office for the interviews. I left only the emergency lights on, plus a low-powered desk lamp. I would sit at her desk, ledger open in front of me, Scott standing behind me. I placed a lone chair in front of the desk.

While we waited for Carolyn to finish her calls, I used another line to call Frank Murphy. He filled us in on the latest at the farm. Cops had found the drugs they had saved from the fire hidden in an old storm cellar. The police had enough evidence to lock all of them up for many years to come. They were talking to their lawyers and not to cops, but Frank exuded confidence about ultimate convictions for those in custody and imminent capture for George and Pete.

Paul and Becky remained in the clear at the moment. The kids had been pretty scared. Frank teased about maybe seeing us on the news. The case seemed pretty weak against some of the people connected with school, except George Windham and Pete Montini. Frank thought a ledger more directly connected to the school might be missing. They'd found ones for all the other local schools among numerous others.

"We'll look through all our stuff and give you a call later if we find anything," I told him.

Frank gave a warning growl, but all he said was "Do that."

Carolyn came into her office. "You guys ready?"

I nodded. Jeff's name topped the list. He shivered as he entered; I suspected it was more from fear than cold. I got him seated. The plan was for Carolyn to wait outside. She was our backup in case of trouble.

"What's going on?" Jeff gave a nervous laugh. "There's a rumor you busted some drug pushers. Did they kill Susan?"

"You lied to us," I said. "You've been pushing drugs at school like everybody else. I want to hear about it, now."

He hung his head and picked at the zipper on his jacket. He told a simple story. He started selling to get a few extra bucks, nothing deliberate, more casual than anything.

"How'd that connect with Susan?" I asked.

"She wasn't dealing, I swear."

"Not that you knew of, anyway," I said. "Who else did she have sex with?"

He shook his head. "Nobody."

"You found out she was screwing anybody with something between his legs, and killed her in a fit of rage."

"No!" he shouted. "Nobody else. She only slept with me. We loved each other."

Scott said, "Then if nobody else had sex with her, it had to be you who made her pregnant."

Jeff clamped his mouth shut. He looked close to tears. Finally, he whispered, "She couldn't have been doing it with anybody else. I'd have known, wouldn't I?" The eternal cry of the odd man out. I felt sorry for him. He didn't kill her. He had no other information for us. We sent him back to the game.

Eric came in next. In contrast to Jeff, he bounced in almost cheerfully. Seated in the chair, hands still bandaged, I saw him betray a squirm, however. His look at us was wary but he still smiled at me.

I was not friendly. "You lied to me," I said. "You've been selling drugs for years. You've been in the center of the whole operation. You've known who and what all along. You jerked us around since the beginning." I watched the cockiness drain from his body.

He started a protest but I cut him off. "You also told me all you did on Wednesday so I'd be suspicious of Becky. You wanted her out of the way, so you could take over her territory. But she found out and turned the tables, and you got a beating. She's tougher than you thought. You knew who beat you up. But yesterday when we talked, you still played a dangerous game. You wanted to get Becky but still not get caught yourself."

"That's bullshit."

I wanted to belt the shit out of him. "And you supplied drugs to Susan and Jeff. And what about your relationship with Susan?"

"I wasn't involved there."

I slammed my fist on the desk. "Spare me your lies. You had sex with her."

"Who said?"

"Does it matter? Is it true?"

In my view, his hesitation condemned him. "And you probably used a goddamn condom."

"I always do when I have sex. But other guys had sex with her. Roger, Paul, lots of guys."

"If you murdered her, we'll find out."

"I didn't kill her," he muttered.

"Who did?" I asked.

He sat up straight in the chair, pointed at me, and said, "You're a real jerk, Mason. I hung around with these guys because the drug business makes me money. Lots of it. I'm not going to be a fucking mechanic all my life. You are the one who got me off the hook for that petty shit, while I dealt drugs in your classroom when your back was turned." He laughed. "What a sap you are."

I didn't know whether he'd killed her or not, but I got no more truth out of him. He left.

Scott said, "Forget his bullshit."

I shrugged. "I've got a murder to solve."

"We didn't learn anything about the murder," Scott pointed out.

Mr. and Mrs. Conlan entered next. Mrs. Conlan marched up to the desk, yelling and pointing her finger at me accusingly. She demanded a lawyer even before we said anything.

"Oh, shut up, Sylvia," Mr. Conlan said. "They aren't cops. We'll answer their questions. We've done nothing illegal, unless protecting our son is a crime. The cops arrested that criminal Jeff Trask. These two investigated. They had no official standing. They wanted to slander our son, ruin his chances for football in college and for a professional career. We took prudent action. They can have no complaints. We didn't obstruct a police investigation. We told the police the truth." He stared at us defiantly from the center of the room.

I said, "You tried to protect your kid with your position on the school board because you thought that even with your clout, if it got into the papers about your kid selling drugs, he'd be gone from the team and out of a career. Sorry, but your son deals and uses drugs, and he's a murder suspect."

Mr. Conlan waved his fist in my face. "You son of a bitch. You have no proof for these accusations."

"Don't I? Your son is free now because of my intervention." I pointed to the ledger. "We've uncovered a vast drug network. He's free because I haven't turned this over to the police yet."

"Let me see that," he demanded.

I held it up to him. He examined where I pointed to Paul's name. He tried to grab it. I held tight and pulled back. I told him I had copies.

"They're fake," he said.

"No. The police have used the ones I left them to arrest a number of bad guys. At the moment, I'm trying to solve a murder. If I don't turn this in, your son may get out of this yet."

He put his fist on his hip and eyed me warily. "Wouldn't you try to protect your son?" He glared at me, expecting an answer. I kept silent.

He continued: "You know the absurd rules they have at this school. If a kid has anything to do with drugs, he's off the team. And colleges won't touch a kid these days if there's the faintest hint of scandal. What did you want me to do?"

I had no answer.

"I couldn't use my position on the board to change the rules. There wasn't time, and it would have been too obvious."

"What did Paul tell you when he got home today?" Scott asked.

I looked to each of them, their pride and defiance shot to hell.

"The police dropped him off at the house only a few minutes before game time. He wouldn't say a word to us. We fought with him. We told him if he didn't talk, he couldn't play in the game. He walked out of the house without a word."

"I almost feel sorry for you," I said, and I meant it.

Several times during the conversation, Mrs. Conlan had said, "Harold, we don't have to listen to these evil men." She said it again now and this time her husband answered. He said, "Oh, shut up, you old fat cow." They stormed out together.

"Does this mean I don't have to go to the opera?" Scott asked.

He and I spoke little as Carolyn left to summon each new person. He held his hurt arm gingerly. I asked him about it. He claimed it didn't hurt. When I thought about it, I could feel my hand and shoulders ache. Occasionally, the remnant of a loud cheer drifted up this far from the gym. Mostly we listened to the onyx clock tick on Carolyn's desk, or stared at the cars in the filled parking lot.

Paul walked in. He looked at us carefully. "It's halftime. I'd like to be back for the end of the game." Paul wore his basketball uniform. On him, it wasn't baggy. His height and muscles filled it powerfully. His tightly held shoulders and clenched fist told of his tension.

"You acted bravely and daringly earlier today," I said. "Brave and foolish, but a friend of yours had died and you were ready to take action. I admire that."

He nodded.

I asked him about drugs. He sat in a chair, head down. He filled in the blanks that there hadn't been time for earlier. In the last couple weeks, he'd felt that Becky had been dragging him in too deep, but he couldn't work up the courage to break away. I asked him about his relationship with Susan.

"She was Jeff's girl. I didn't really know her."

"She was pregnant. Did you ever have sex with her?"

He slowly looked up. "No. Yeah. Who said I did?"

I gazed at him evenly.

He hung his head. "Yeah, I did. The other guys said she was wild, fun, and willing. Why not? Only once, though. And I used a condom. But Becky was my girl. She was"—he said the next in a low voice to the rug—"more than enough for me."

Another candidate for the Surgeon General's award list. "Why didn't you tell me everything that first night?"

"I didn't want to be involved. I was afraid I'd be reported to the administration and thrown off the team. It would have ruined my chances for a good college program."

"We talked to your parents about that," I said.

"They tried to pressure me when I got home. I may quit the team. All they can think of is cover up, ignore it. I can't do that. I fucked up. I saw Becky when I got to school tonight. She told me anything I didn't know about the drug operation and the people involved. I was blind to so much." He paused, shook his head. "I have a question for you. Why haven't they arrested me? I dealt drugs, although I didn't tell the cops about that this afternoon. I must have been in the ledgers."

"We're trying to find the murderer. We're using the River's Edge one as leverage to get answers."

He smiled weakly. "Good idea."

I explained that we had no desire to ruin his chances for a pro career with the drug information. He squared his shoulders at that and looked less pale and distracted.

I watched him stride out with the grace and assurance of a natural athlete.

After he left, I said, "I feel sorry for Susan. None of these people seemed to care about her or really know her. I'm convinced one of them did it."

"Evidence? Proof?" Scott let the words dangle.

"No," I admitted.

Carolyn entered. We told her what had happened. She said, "You guys have done the district and the kids a big favor in busting this drug business. Let the police handle the murder now. You've done as much as you can."

Minutes later, we trudged down toward the gym. The hall lights flicked out as we passed the science room. A gun, followed by a hand and arm, emerged from the doorway. "Into the room," George's voice said.

Masses of test tubes neatly lined up and microscopes encased in plastic rested on the rows of neatly arranged black lab tables.

Charts with every aspect of the human anatomy exposed lined the walls.

Pete stood out from the deepest shadows. He looked miserably disheveled, cold, and wet. George's left arm hung almost lifelessly. The muzzle of the gun in his right hand stared at us mercilessly.

I gazed from one to the other. "Why Pete?" I asked.

The light from a streetlamp outside shone on Pete's baldness. I watched his scowl and his shivers. He stomped over to us and shoved a finger in my face. "You bastards." His face was close enough that I could confirm his reputation for dragon breath. "Paul Conlan was my ticket out of this hole. He's one of the ten top prospects in the country in football and basketball. I've had offers from two major colleges. If I could take the kid with me, they'd give me a job. Your fucking investigation threatened my whole future. I tried to protect the kid from any taint of scandal. You stupid shits. I didn't want murder. I want the good life like you've got.

"So I chased you around town. I covered for Paul when he came to me with all the drug stuff. He didn't know how involved I was at the time. Nothing I did worked. It got out of control."

George said, "Enough bullshit. You've got a ledger I need. Give or you die, and I want the copies I presume you made."

"How'd you know we had them?"

"We had a state police cop bought, too. He got to you too late because of the snow. We called him. He told us."

I handed him the ledger. "The police have enough on you without this," I said. "And one copy's in the mail."

"We'll deal with that later. This is a start." In the dim light, he glanced over the ledger. Finally, he said, "But the police will have a lot less when I destroy this." George gave an ugly laugh. "We'll go to your house to check for more copies. We had a nice little operation. Ready to move into the big time. I think we'll burn your little bungalow with the two of you in it. A little revenge could be good for your growth as human beings."

He motioned us toward the corner of the room near the door. We huddled exactly where he shouldn't have put us. Each classroom has an intercom button near the door. As we leaned together, I pressed my elbow against it. Being in the newest section of the school raised the odds on the damn thing actually working. I braced myself to spring at the moment of distraction when the intercom clicked on. Pete slowly opened the door. I pictured the office and heard the intercom buzz in my mind as I'd heard it a hundred times. I prayed Carolyn was still in the office.

"Hall's clear," Pete said.

With the point of the gun, George urged us forward. The intercom clicked on. Carolyn's voice said, "Is someone there?"

George screamed as I yanked his gun arm up and rammed my knee into his nuts. Scott jumped Pete. Even with one arm encumbered by the cast, he subdued him in a moment.

Help arrived in the form of Carolyn and a phalanx of janitors. We didn't wait for the police to come and take them. Instead, we finished our journey to the gym. We found seats in the top row of the bleachers only because two freshmen were too polite or scared of a teacher to refuse to move. Scott remained unrecognized, the crowd being intent on the last minutes of the game. We watched an assistant coach try to ease the boys into a win. The game was against Joliet Central, a power in the state this year. Our side seemed disorganized. Without Jeff, the team was hurting, but Paul wasn't in top form, either. That was understandable given what had happened to him. In the last two minutes, however, they looked as if they'd pull it together. From a five-point deficit, they rallied.

The bleachers rocked with noise. The rafters echoed and reechoed the crowd's joy as the team pulled ahead by one, fell behind again, then ahead. The place was all noise, people, and light. However, in the last half minute, the team fell apart. First, one of our guys traveled. Then Paul muffed an easy inbounds pass. Then another teammate threw the ball into the arms of an opponent. We lost by a bucket.

I sat with chin cupped in hand watching the chastened crowd exit. As the last fans trickled out, Becky entered the gym, saw us, and climbed up. As she ascended, the bleachers echoed with the stomps of her feet.

"I'm going to hate you forever," she announced loudly from the step below us.

"We saved your life," Scott said.

"Who cares? They didn't arrest me."

"That's because I kept the ledger that implicates you. I intend to show it to the police."

She started screaming. "I wish I'd killed you Tuesday night. Paul wrenched the wheel out of my hand at the last second. The bastard saved you. Now all he cares about is saving his precious career." She snorted. "Poor innocent Paul. Wise old Becky had to fill him in on the way the world really works." She lowered her voice to almost normal. "He broke up with me tonight. It's your fault." She drew a deep breath. "I bet even with that ledger they won't do anything to me. Fuck you. You're bluffing."

"Are you really that stupid?" I asked.

Scott stood up. His deep voice rumbled. "Leave before I throw you through the basketball hoop from here."

She hesitated a second, recognized the genuine menace in his voice, and retreated. We got a few more choice obscenities shouted at us before she blasted out the doors.

I remained seated. Scott sat back down. Later, a few custodians swept the floor and still I sat. Scott put a hand on my shoulder. "You did your best," he said. "Let's go home and forget it. The danger to us is over. My arm's starting to hurt, and you must still be stiff and sore from the other night."

"I want to stay a little longer," I said.

He let me alone, didn't ask questions. The custodians finished.

They looked up at where we sat. I gave a brief wave to one whom I recognized, but didn't speak to him. They doused the lights, leaving only red exit signs lit. That and light from the hallway flowing through the glass in the doors seeped in. The heat dissipated slowly. I looked through the squares of window twenty feet above. Light from a half-moon streamed in, forming soft patches of brightness near us. Still I sat. The locker-room noises faded. No sound came from the hallway.

We heard the handle of a door click.

⑪

A figure emerged from the boys' locker room. He carried a gym bag and moved slowly. We were out of the moonlight, in deepest shadows. The figure trudged across the darkened gym floor. He passed through a square of brightness, but I couldn't make out who it was.

He stopped directly below where we sat. He looked up, then began to ascend. Slow measured steps, each one seeming to take minutes, brought him to where we sat. Up the tiers he came, stopping three rows below us. He sat in a patch of moonlight, straddling the bleacher seat. He placed his gym bag on the seat between his knees.

He looked up. It was Paul Conlan. He wore faded blue jeans, white socks, gym shoes, and a white sweater. He placed his winter coat on his gym bag.

He sighed. He fiddled with the straps on the gym bag.

At last, he said, "I saw you guys up here at the end of the game."

"Becky told us about you breaking up with her," I said.

"She's a fucking bitch." For a moment, he seemed to inflate with anger, then almost as quickly shrank back within himself. When he spoke, more teenage pathos filled his voice than I could imagine possible. "She laughed at me when she told me about how she ran everything. How she had people beaten up.

She laughed at Roger being dead. She said I was so naïve. I know nobody else liked her, but I loved her. We'd been going together since grade school. I knew she did stupid stuff, and I knew what I did was wrong, but I didn't know how rotten she was." He pushed his gym bag a few feet down the bench. He made a fist, then rapped his knuckles softly on the polished wood.

"I'm sorry about Becky," I said. And I found it was true. I felt sorry for the kid and her screwed-up life.

Minutes dragged by in silence. Finally, I said, "Tough game. Hard one to lose."

"Thanks. We should have won." Again silence ticked by.

"Everybody else gone?" I asked.

"Yeah. I was the last one out of the locker room." He stared at the moonlight that streamed through the windows far and high above. "Mr. Mason?"

"Yeah?"

"I killed her."

Perhaps my heart stopped. Certainly the world and time paused for me.

"I did have sex with her, but I lied. I didn't use protection. She came back Sunday night. Everybody was gone. She was hurt from her fight with Jeff. She told me she was pregnant, that I was the father. Something snapped in me.

"Becky constantly pressured me for more sex, to be more involved in drugs. Susan was free, easy, no hassle. With her, I felt calm. But the pressure was too much! My mom and dad constantly pushed me in sports. They wanted a sports hero for a son. Since I was eleven, it was always more, more, win, hurt the other guys. I hate them! I hate the pressure.

"Coach Montini made it worse. I was his ticket out of here. I don't know how many times he told me that. I was his first real pro prospect. Job opportunities would open up. He hated being a high school coach."

He shoved his gym bag farther away. His voice stayed low,

almost clinical. "So when Susan told me she was pregnant, I couldn't take it. I could never marry her. She cried and whimpered. I held her while I seethed and my hatred grew. We did some coke and we began having sex. I was rough with her. "She . . ." He paused. "She liked it. She begged for more. I don't know what came over me. I lost control. I killed her."

He stopped and drew a deep breath. He didn't burst into tears. Moonlight shone on his damp blond hair. He continued in his soft voice. I could barely hear him.

"Poor Jeff. I'm sorry I got him in trouble. I wish I could have been the friend he wanted." He paused a minute, then continued. "I always thought of myself as a normal guy. A good athlete. I like kids looking up to me, liking me. But then I always had to be that for everybody: kids, teachers, coaches, parents. It felt like the whole world was watching me every minute. I wanted to be a pro athlete, a star. But each new pressure was like another noose around my neck."

"I understand," Scott said.

Paul glanced at him. "Yeah, you would, Mr. Carpenter. I wished I'd met you sooner to talk about it. Anyway, I couldn't handle it. And now . . ." He sighed deepest of all. "Now it's all useless."

Two nights later, we lay side by side next to Scott's Christmas tree. Christmas Eve at my younger brother's had been beautiful. Scott had sat cross-legged on the floor in front of the fireplace, all the little kids in their pajamas surrounding him, the littlest one sheltered in his lap. He had read story after story until they all fell asleep.

My family's that morning and afternoon had been a wonderful chaotic Christmas: yelling kids and parents, warm closeness. At five, the doorbell had rung.

Scott's sister had tracked us down. She and Scott had retired to my parents' bedroom and talked for two hours. They came out misty-eyed and arm in arm.

Yesterday morning, I'd talked with Frank Murphy. He said they'd gotten the whole story from Paul. He almost felt sorry for the kid. They'd arrested Becky and Eric. He told me I was right about Becky. She'd been more trouble than any three people with whom he'd ever dealt. Mysteriously, another ledger had turned up. He said, "You know, Tom, some of the people we talked to claim you threatened them with a ledger."

"I lied," I said. "There was an extra blank ledger in the stack. While we waited in the gas station, I made up names and figures and wrote them in. I mixed in some real stuff from the ledgers to make it look real. They bought my bluff." We'd left the ledger book in the police station mailbox and called in an anonymous tip. I'd wiped my fingerprints off carefully. Frank had sounded unconvinced by my explanation, but he let it go.

With one finger, I slowly traced the outline of Scott's muscles on his chest and shoulders. We had only the tree lights on. Judy Collins sang "Who Knows Where the Time Goes." I felt the same goose bumps I had when I first heard her sing that song.

"I'm glad my sister came," Scott said. "She thinks Mom and Dad will come around."

"That's great," I said.

I rested my hand on his chest. It rose and fell with his breathing. The song ended. Silence filled the penthouse. I smelled the pine needles from the tree and the apple wood in the fireplace. Outdoors, the temperature, after a brief rise the day before, was on its way down to another record low. I watched snow swirl outside the windows. "We could be trapped here until the end of the next ice age," I said.

"I can't think of anyone I'd rather spend the time with," he said.

A few minutes before, we'd exchanged Christmas presents. For me, he'd gotten a signed first-edition set of Tolkien's *Lord of the Rings*. I'd spent nearly a year talking to his junior high and high school coaches and getting as many videos of his games put together as I could. Meg had proved invaluable in helping to get tapes from his parents. I'd had copies made and sent the originals back. Some were nearly twenty-five years old. He nearly cried when he stuck it in the VCR and realized what it was.

I leaned over and kissed him gently on the lips. I said, "I love you."